T0054196

the Crimson Key

SECOND EDITION

the Crimson Key

Wes Dodd

TATE PUBLISHING
AND **ENTERPRISES,** LLC

The Crimson Key
Copyright © 2014 by Wes Dodd. All rights reserved.

No part of this publication may be reproduced, stored in a retrieval system or transmitted in any way by any means, electronic, mechanical, photocopy, recording or otherwise without the prior permission of the author except as provided by USA copyright law.

This novel is a work of fiction. Names, descriptions, entities, and incidents included in the story are products of the author's imagination. Any resemblance to actual persons, events, and entities is entirely coincidental.

The opinions expressed by the author are not necessarily those of Tate Publishing, LLC.

Published by Tate Publishing & Enterprises, LLC
127 E. Trade Center Terrace | Mustang, Oklahoma 73064 USA
1.888.361.9473 | www.tatepublishing.com

Tate Publishing is committed to excellence in the publishing industry. The company reflects the philosophy established by the founders, based on Psalm 68:11,
"The Lord gave the word and great was the company of those who published it."

Book design copyright © 2014 by Tate Publishing, LLC. All rights reserved.
Cover design by Junriel Boquecosa
Interior design by Jomel Pepito

Published in the United States of America

ISBN: 978-1-62994-640-5
1. Fiction / Mystery & Detective / Cozy
2. Fiction / Mystery & Detective / General
14.01.14

Acknowledgment

A special thanks and dedication goes to Pamela Bates. She has a special way of touching every life she comes in contact with. Her encouragement and enthusiasm touched my heart, fueling my passion to write.

I would like to thank Jon Marken, great job editing and a pleasure to work with.

Special thanks go to my two daughters, Tina and Lesley. Their enthusiasm kept me on the path to publishing my first novel.

Though they knew nothing of my endeavor, I would like to thank my parents, Bernice and Franklin. They have always been there for me on this rocky road I call my life.

Chapter 1

On a dark mid-November night in 1986, rain fell hard from the black sky above, rain bitterly cold like liquid ice. The fierce wind whipped it in sheets, punishing anything in its path. On the outskirts of Philadelphia in a suburban neighborhood, a fiery red Z28 slowly pulled to a curb in front of a small three-bedroom, single-story brick house. The driver, a distraught young woman, slowly leaned forward, resting her head on the leather-covered steering wheel. She cried uncontrollably. A few minutes passed before she finally reached up and turned off the ignition, silencing the motor and radio just as Michael Jackson's Thriller was ending. She sat up straight once again, wiping her face in an attempt to regain her composure for the clandestine mission ahead of her. She cast a pair of glassy eyes to her right, drawn to a small basket much like a picnic basket in the dark leather seat beside her. While she gazed relentlessly at the basket, she realized once again that she had made the right decision.

Alice Paige rose up in her bed, awakened by a pounding on her door. She peered at the clock—1:07 a.m. She carefully placed her book on the nightstand, the book she was reading when she drifted off. "Who is at my door at one in the morning?" she thought to herself as she slipped on her heavy brown robe. Reaching the front door, she pulled the curtain back carefully, just enough to peek outside. Though the front was dimly lit and the rain poured down, she instantly recognized the figure that stood on her front stoop. The long blonde hair and familiar curvatures of her slender face could be but one person. Alice slowly opened the door and invited her twin sister, Amber, inside.

Alice and Amber were identical twins at birth, though now complete opposites in many ways. Alice had light ash brown hair that she kept very short. She never wore makeup and was considered plain-looking and ordinary in her ways. Amber, on the other hand, was gifted with rare beauty and a voluptuous figure. She did very well in beauty pageants and at age eighteen went off to New York City in pursuit of a modeling career. Alice remained hidden in her shadow.

Amber entered slowly, carrying an odd-looking basket covered entirely with a blue blanket, wet from the rain. She tugged a large suitcase on wheels that seemed to be very heavy. She sat the basket down gingerly, as if what lay hidden within might be fragile. Amber then fell into her sister's arms, releasing a flood of emotions. She hugged Alice tightly, clinging firmly to her as if hanging on for dear life. The two were very close as young children but grew farther and farther apart with each passing year. Amber had blossomed rapidly, leaving Alice behind in a life filled with neglect, which led to resentment on her part. Alice felt and heard her sister sobbing for the first time she could remember.

"Why are you crying?" Alice asked tenderly.

"Alice," Amber replied in a shaky voice, then hesitated a long moment. "You do know that I have always loved you dearly, don't you?"

"Why of course," Alice promptly replied, while she thought to herself, "You sure have a funny way of showing it. I only see you about once a year, and it is always at night so no one will recognize you coming here. We never go out together in public. You make me feel as if you are ashamed to be seen with me." Then Alice asked in a caring way, "What is wrong?"

Amber made a good effort to gather her emotions as she released her hold on Alice. Taking a step back, she wiped the tears from her face. "I am in love with an evil man."

Alice didn't feel sorry for her at first, or the least bit shocked by her statement. She thought to herself again, "I'm not surprised. You have always chosen the wrong type men. You always pursued the Bad Boys, or what you would call the Fun Guys."

Then Alice noticed a bruise on Amber's left cheek, and her feelings changed instantly. She asked in a serious tone, "What is his name?"

Alice and Amber stood facing, eyes locked in a stare, Alice waiting for an answer that Amber did not want to reveal. A tiny whimper then broke their stare. Alice's eyes dropped instantly to the basket below that remained mysteriously covered with the blue blanket. The basket moved ever so slightly as another tiny whimper came from within. Alice's eyes rose quickly, meeting Amber's, which were again overflowing with tears.

"What have you got?" Alice asked very slowly as she knelt down next to the basket. She gently rolled back the blanket revealing a tiny, tiny baby boy.

"I couldn't do it," Amber said in a trembling voice, as tears rolled rapidly down her cheeks.

Alice could hear her sister's voice but failed to comprehend a single word; the tiny baby boy had stolen her full attention.

"I kept it a secret for as long as I could," Amber continued. "I knew he didn't want a child, him being married with a child on the way and due at any time now. At least it was when I left three days ago. It would have made him very angry…and he has a furious temper."

"What is his name?" Alice asked while kissing the tiny baby's forehead as she cradled him in her loving arms.

"It would be best if you didn't know. Anyway, he doesn't even know that you exist. And now that is a good thing."

"No…not the idiot," Alice responded. "This beautiful little angel lying in my arms."

"David," Amber replied, and then hesitated for a few moments. "I couldn't bring myself to do it."

Memories flooded Alice's mind, memories that had haunted her for years. Three years before, Alice was two weeks from marrying the man of her dreams. She was also five months pregnant. In the blink of an eye her life was drastically changed forever. On a night much like this one, just before the holiday season, a drunk driver crossed the yellow line. The last thing Alice remembered was bright lights, followed quickly by screeching tires. When she regained consciousness three long days later, she opened her eyes to a living nightmare. Her once well-planned life had instantly transformed into a never-ending heartache. Her fiancé was killed instantly when the drunk driver plowed head first into their compact car. The innocent child she had carried for five months unfortunately would never see her mother's smiling face. Just when Alice thought that life could not get any worse, she got some terrible news. Due to her extensive injuries that crushed her pelvis, she would never be able to bear children.

"What couldn't you do?" Alice asked, as she returned to reality.

After a long moment of silence and no apparent answer to her question, Alice drew her eyes away from little David and raised them towards Amber. When their eyes finally met, Alice instantly knew the answer to her question, as if it was written on Amber's face. Alice's eyes widened and her face turned pale at the thought, astonishment mixed with anguish. Stunned and speechless, she stared into Amber's tear-stained eyes. After a long moment of silence, their stare was broken by little David's attempt to wrap his tiny little hand around Alice's pinky finger. The timing was perfect, and his touch melted her heart. Alice turned her full attention to the baby. She imagined that little David had actually given her a smile, and tears filled her eyes as joy filled her face. The love for a child is instantaneous and uncontrollable. But his touch went much deeper than mere love; it pierced her soul and thus an unbreakable bond was born.

"I could never do anything like that," Amber reassured Alice. "You have to believe me. He thinks that I am away terminating the pregnancy...and he threatened me."

"So that's how you got that bruise," Alice remarked. She walked to the sofa, carefully taking a seat, her eyes then turning towards the large suitcase on wheels. "And now you have come here because you are on the run. And you wish to move in with me, away from this evil tyrant."

"Yes," Amber quickly replied, then hesitated— "and no."

Alice slowly raised her eyes to meet Amber's. A look of puzzlement accompanied her stare. They looked at one another for what seemed like an eternity. Then almost as if Alice could read her sister's mind, she suddenly realized why Amber had come. "Could this be the answer to my question I have been asking for years?" Alice thought to herself. She had been questioning God as to why her life was spared on that tragic day three years ago. What possible reason could God have for putting her through such misery? Then she had a strange epiphany, and thought to herself, "This is why God spared my life, to save little David's.

Yes, that is it—David will fill the void I have had the past three years."

Amber slowly sat on the sofa by Alice, her misty eyes never wavering. "If I go back…he will kill us both," Amber said through tear-filled eyes. "If I don't go back…then he will not give up until he finds us both. This affair and little David threaten his career. This is the only way to be absolutely sure that David will be safe…that is if I give him to you."

Alice's heart swelled and eyes soon followed, filling rapidly with tears of joy.

"You know that I love David with all my heart," Amber said tearfully. "That is why I have to do this. It is the only way…the only reason I could ever give him away…and only to you…my dear, dear Alice."

Alice was too choked up to speak, as if her heart was stuck in her throat, so she nodded to let Amber know that she understood. "But what about you?" Alice finally asked.

Amber stared into Alice's glassy eyes for a few moments. And without answering the question she turned her head as her eyes absorbed everything in the room, until they finally landed on the mantle filled with pictures. Silently she rose, slowly walking to the mantle as if the mantle was mysteriously drawing her to it. Her eyes first fell upon a picture of a pretty teenage girl, the mother she never knew, who was robbed of life at the young age of sixteen while giving birth to twins. "This is the greatest…no the only selfless thing that I have ever done. And probably the only thing I have ever done out of pure love."

Amber then reached up, taking down a frame with her grandmother's picture inside, who raised both Amber and Alice from birth. It had been only a year since cancer took her away. Tears ran slowly down Amber's cheeks as she ran her hand across the glass. "Have you ever had a feeling deep down inside…that you would never see or return to a place ever again? And wished that you could go back in time to relive it again, appreciating it for what it was?"

Alice did not give her an answer, but glanced back and forth between Amber and little David, trying to figure out the strange way her sister was acting.

"Hey Sis," Amber said, and then waited intentionally for Alice to answer.

"Yes," Alice eventually replied, thinking it strange she called her Sis as she had not heard that word since they were children.

"I wish that I had been more like you," Amber remarked.

Alice remained silent, but thoughts raced through her mind. "What! You have always thought only of yourself. You have always known that you were beautiful and special. And you made sure that I knew it too."

"If I was only more like you," Amber continued as she stared at a picture of Alice and herself at Christmas when they were only seven, "Then my life would not be in the mess it is now. I am twenty-five years old, and the only thing that I have ever done that turned out good in my life is David."

Amber turned, facing Alice who held little David securely in her arms. A smile grew slowly on Amber's face at the precious sight, and then tears rolled down her cheeks as she returned to the sofa. She gently took a seat by Alice. "This is the only way to make absolutely sure that David will be safe. You are going to think that I'm crazy because the idea came to me in a dream, by an angel of all things."

Alice looked up at Amber; astonishment filled her face.

"I know what you are thinking," Amber said without hesitation. "I was just as shocked as you. I have never given religion or God much thought, even though Ma Mama," which was what they both called their grandmother, "took us to Sunday school every Sunday. But now I do…and I want to do the right thing for David, not myself. He is a little miracle being weeks early and only three pounds three ounces. Even though he is a preemie, the doctor said that he is very strong and healthy. He does not anticipate any problems with him that a little TLC will not take care of."

Amber rose and walked slowly to the large suitcase, then pulled it back to Alice's feet. "This suitcase doesn't have my belongings inside. It's money that I took from David's father, for you and David. I know what you must be thinking. I don't think of it as stealing, but rather what is rightfully David's anyway. There is enough money inside to last you the rest of your life if managed properly, like I know you will do."

"What about you?" Alice asked out of concern. "What will happen to you?"

Amber didn't answer, but instead reached up behind her neck with both hands. She unclasped the silver chain that hung down resting comfortably within her cleavage. She then pulled the necklace out from under her red dress, revealing on the other end a red crimson-colored key.

"If I become missing...or worse," Amber said somberly, "this key will answer all your questions, and any mysteries including my demise."

Chapter 2

25 Years Later

Alice Paige, a handsome lady of fifty, walked happily up Rose Lane to her job at the nearby Village Library in beautiful Mount Pleasant, the town Alice thought must have gotten its name due to the pleasant weather year round. Mount Pleasant is a rapidly growing suburban town of Charleston, South Carolina. Alice moved there twenty-five years ago, escaping the cold winters of Philadelphia and whatever dangers involved David's father.

Alice loved her job dearly, for reading books had always been her passion. She took the job when David was old enough to enter school, with a very flexible schedule arranged for any and all activities that David participated in, since he was Alice's sole purpose in life. David had never been the type teenager that went into every sport or activity. Other than his grades, he focused on one other thing and one thing only, golf. He excelled in the sport, becoming the number one seed on his high school team, the Wando High School Warriors, which earned him a full scholarship to the University of South Carolina. He graduated four years later with a Bachelor's Degree in Criminology and Criminal Justice and became a detective for the Charleston County Sheriff's Department.

This particular day Alice proudly wore a huge smile, because this Sunday was little David's twenty-fifth birthday. But he was by no means very little any more, standing a half inch over six feet, lean and very toned. Alice had been wearing that smile continuously for the past twenty-five years, a completely different person from the one before her twin sister arrived. Her life changed considerably for the better when David entered in, and no one in Mount Pleasant would ever suspect that behind that continuous smile lay a deep secret. Not even David suspected a thing. The secret was not supposed to go on this long; Amber had asked Alice to tell David the truth when he became an adult, and give him the crimson key. Alice had not seen or heard anything from her twin sibling since, and still she kept the secret from David for her own selfish reasons, even though it was out of love.

Sunday, November 13th, began at about fifty degrees, warming up nicely to sixty-six, perfect golf weather. A birthday party was planned at the golf club for six in the evening, after David's Sunday round with his buddies. Alice had this planned for two months now, with the help of his lady friend, Kimberly Wells. Kimberly had been David's high school sweetheart. But their relationship grew cold while he was off at college and she went to nursing school. After David settled back in the area, they saw each other often, romantically that is. Though each did not date other people, neither did either one make a full commitment to the other. So therefore they were involved in an uncomplicated relationship.

As David entered the banquet room from the lounge, Kimberly intercepted him at the door. "And where do you think you are going?" she asked, as she stared into his piercing blue eyes. "You are not supposed to be here until six."

David stared back into her sensuous green eyes. "It's not a surprise party."

She playfully pushed him back into the lobby. "Still, the guest of honor is not supposed to arrive before the other guests."

Kimberly's smile aroused David. He grabbed her lovingly and pulled her around the corner out of sight. Pressing gently against her petite body, he planted a kiss on her luscious lips. Surrendering easily, she wrapped her arms around him, running her fingers through his light ash brown hair, melting into the kiss. David slowly and tenderly ran his hands up her nursing top, cleverly unbuttoning his way up. He reached the last one on top before she realized what he was doing. "What are you doing?" she asked, breathlessly whispering into his ear.

"Unwrapping my birthday gift," he replied while tickling her ear with his tongue.

"You will just have to wait," she responded while buttoning up her top. "Now go fix you a drink in the lounge. Watch some football or something…just don't come back until six." She gave him a quick kiss on the lips. "If you are one minute early…you will not get your birthday gift."

He gave her a grin as she turned and entered the door to the banquet room, her petite five-foot-four frame and short blonde hair etched in his mind. David returned five minutes after six, not taking a chance on being early. He was intercepted at the door once again, only this time by his mother's smiling face. "Happy birthday," Alice said as she pulled him down, placing a kiss on his right cheek.

David returned her kiss on the cheek and then gave her a tight bear hug. The room was spacious with an area in the front center for dancing. Tables with chairs for six filled the opposite side and rear of the room, with thirty of David's closest friends from work and golf already occupying the seats. A local DJ cranked up the music as guests began to pour onto the dance floor. David slowly made his way around the room and then onto the dance floor, greeting all his friends. Before he could escape the dance floor, a hand grabbed his belt from the rear, pulling him back to the middle of the floor. He turned around suddenly, falling helplessly into Kimberly's arms. After a seductive kiss, they broke out in dance. David gazed at her as reflections of bright colors from the spinning disco light in the ceiling drowned her white uniform.

After several hours of partying, and a couple requested slow dances with her son, Alice approached David. "I hate to be a party pooper," Alice said as she suffered a smile at him with his arm on Kimberly's shoulders, "but my migraine has returned with a vengeance. I had better go home and go to bed."

David hugged Alice tightly. "Thanks, Mom...this was the best party ever."

"You say that every year," she responded, while giving Kimberly a hug as well. "I love you, Son."

"Love you too, Mom," he responded as he carefully watched her walk away.

Kimberly saw the worry painted on his face. "What's wrong?"

David hesitated, not answering for his eyes were fixed on his mom. She had been sick before and most definitely had had these recurring migraines, but he had a sense of worry he hadn't felt before and couldn't explain why. After she disappeared through the door, he replied, "I'm worried about her migraines."

"Has she seen a doctor?"

"No," he replied. "I can't get her to see one. She thinks that the only thing the doctor will do is dope her up unnecessarily and waste her money."

"That is silly," Kimberly remarked. "When was the last time she had a checkup?"

David's eyes narrowed as he tried to think back. The only time he could recollect seeing her at a doctor was when she had taken him. "I have never known her to see a doctor."

"Not even for a mammogram?" she asked as shock covered her face.

David shook his head slowly. "Nope...I don't think so," he finally replied. "And she just turned fifty."

"I tell you what," Kimberly said. "I will talk to her this week."

David took Kimberly's hand. "That would mean a lot to me."

"Consider that a birthday gift," she said, and then a grin grew on her face.

"Wait just a minute," he said as he pulled her up close. "You can't take back a gift that I have already started unwrapping."

"Is that you talking? Or the Captain Morgan?" she asked. Then their eyes met and they fell instantly into a sensuous kiss.

The next afternoon after her shift at Charleston Memorial Hospital, Kimberly paid Alice a visit. She knocked, and Alice invited her in. "Why do you still knock on my door?" Alice asked. "You know you are like my own daughter."

Kimberly smiled and gave Alice a hug. "You are just the sweetest woman I have ever known." She pulled back, looking Alice directly into her eyes. "I am worried."

"Don't give up on David...I know he loves you deeply," Alice said seriously.

Kimberly smiled and hugged her again. "No... David is worried too."

"Worried about what?" Alice asked as she pulled back to look Kimberly in her eyes.

"You," Kimberly replied, taking Alice by her hand.

"Oh, good grief," Alice responded, releasing Kimberly's hand while walking towards the kitchen. "Would you like something to drink while you wait for David?"

Kimberly followed. "I came here to see you."

Alice opened the refrigerator, bringing out a pitcher of sweet tea. "Would you like some lemon?" she asked, avoiding any talk about her health.

"No thank you," Kimberly replied. "You appear to be a picture of health, but it wouldn't hurt to get a checkup."

"Is this about my migraines?" Alice asked as she poured the tea.

"Not entirely," she replied. "Everyone, especially women, should have checkups periodically. I'm only twenty-five, but I get a checkup every year."

David arrived and walked into the kitchen. "Well looky here…my two favorite women in the whole wide world," he said as he stared not at them but at the glasses of sweet tea.

"Did you put her up to this?" Alice asked as she handed him a glass of tea.

"Hey," David said, and then put his hands in the air. "She is on her own."

Kimberly rose quickly, chasing him around the table. David grabbed his mother, using her as a shield from Kimberly. "But if you don't hurry up and agree," David said, "she is going to kill me."

"Okay," Alice said. "I guess it wouldn't hurt to get a checkup. I will make an appointment tomorrow. But only because it will save your butt."

"Thanks Mom," David responded, releasing her and taking a sip out of Kimberly's glass of tea.

"Hey!" Kimberly yelled. "My glass was full." Kimberly walked up to David and punched him on his arm, jostling some tea out the glass onto his shirt.

Alice laughed out loud. "What do my two favorite children want for supper?"

David and Kimberly instantly locked eyes, answering at the same time, "Pizza!"

Alice shook her head. "I should have known."

Chapter 3

Alice had a restless night, not from a migraine but rather from dreams. Alice had not seen her twin sister Amber's face for twenty-five years now, until this night. The first dream was very short, awakening her quickly at the first sight of Amber. Alice rose out of bed and put on her turquoise blue robe as she headed to the kitchen. It was only a little after eleven and David was still up watching the news.

"Can't sleep?" David asked, watching Alice walk through silently, as if sleep walking. After not getting an answer he rose out of the recliner and headed to the kitchen. Quietly entering the kitchen, he found Alice at the sink staring out the window into the darkness, as if in a trance. He walked up to Alice, placing a hand on her shoulder. She jumped at his touch. "Mom...are you okay?"

"Yes," she replied with her hand on her heart. "I didn't hear you come in."

"I asked you a question when you came through the living room," he said as he looked into her distant eyes. "Are you sure you are okay?"

"Yes Honey," she replied with a smile. "Been reading too much I guess."

"You still reading that last Harry Potter book?"

"No," she replied as she opened the refrigerator, taking out a container of milk. "I finished that two weeks ago. That was a great series."

"Now are you ready to watch the movies?"

She smiled at him. "No thank you…the books are always better."

"Not possible," he responded, "especially with the last one. If you are sure that you are okay, then I will be turning in."

She sat at the table with a glass of milk. "I'm fine…sleep tight."

Alice sipped on her milk while thoughts raced through her mind. Thoughts of the last time she saw Amber and whatever happened to her. Guilt overcame her as a single tear rolled down her cheek. "I should have searched for her," Alice thought to herself. "But I couldn't risk it. No, I couldn't take that chance," she reasoned with herself. "Amber wanted me to protect David…and that is what I did. So why is she coming to me in my dream? Why now after twenty-five years?" She took the last swallow of milk. "Maybe she is trying to tell me something," she thought as she rinsed out the glass. "But what could it be?"

Alice returned to bed, then turned out the light. She tossed and turned continuously until finally she surrendered and drifted slowly into dreamland, a place she visited regularly as she entered into whatever story she was reading about. As she began to dream, she returned to her home in Philadelphia. Alice relived the entire visit from Amber, from the surprising beginning to the heartfelt gift Amber brought her, and then the sad but inevitable departure, never to see her twin sibling again. The moment Amber gave her the crimson key, she woke again. Alice cast an eye towards her clock on the nightstand, 3 a.m. She slowly rose out of bed and headed towards the chest of drawers. Alice reached down, opening the bottom drawer. She dug through the drawer to the back, then suddenly stopped, pulling out the silver necklace with the crimson key dangling on the end. Alice held the chain up, staring intensely at the key. She then walked slowly back to bed and sat on the edge, opening the drawer on the nightstand. Pulling out a white business envelope, she carefully placed the necklace inside. Reaching in the drawer again, she pulled out a writing pad. She sat up comfortably in bed, as she always did when reading, but instead of reading, she began to write.

The next day Alice made two appointments, one with a doctor for a checkup after Thanksgiving, the other with a lawyer for that afternoon. Alice had intense migraines the next three afternoons.

Friday, Alice took her lunch break and read a book as usual, while also picking at a salad. As she was chewing while reading, she bit her tongue. She instantly closed her eyes, trying to deal with the pain. She began to feel dizzy and opened her eyes. The words on the page of the book became blurred. Alice shut her eyes once again, holding them shut for several minutes. Her dizziness left as quickly as it came. Slowly she opened her eyes, finding the words on the page intact. Shaken, she rose to her feet, but all felt normal once again. Frightened as never before, Alice took off the rest of the day with sick leave and drove to Charleston Memorial Hospital.

Kimberly was just finishing her lunch break when she spotted Alice at the end of the hall near the main lobby. She called Alice by name and headed in her direction. Alice did not respond to Kimberly's calling, but instead stood staring straight ahead, as if dazed. Kimberly sensed something wrong, so she quickened her pace. Just as she got within several arm lengths of Alice, Alice turned her stare to Kimberly. The cold look on her face frightened Kimberly. Then Alice fell helplessly to the floor, dropping as if all the life from her was suddenly gone. Kimberly frantically called for help while checking Alice's vitals. After securely in the hands of several doctors, Kimberly called David.

Twenty minutes later, David and Kimberly embraced in the waiting room. David could feel Kimberly's tears as his cheek caressed hers. "What happened?"

Kimberly pulled back and looked into his eyes. "I'm not sure. She was standing near the lobby just staring out into space. Just as I was getting near her, she turned and looked at me. Then she just fell to the floor. She had a frightened look on her face like I have never seen before."

"Something was wrong with her last night," he responded. "I caught her gazing out the kitchen window into the darkness. She said she was all right, so I went to bed." David was suddenly overwhelmed with guilt. He felt as if he let her down when all his life she had taken good care of him with a loving hand. They shared a special relationship, closer than normal because she tended to his every need and was always there for him. She could always sense when something was wrong even if it was just something on his mind. "Why couldn't he see this coming?" he scolded himself.

About that time, a tall thin dark-skinned man wearing a hair net walked in, instantly making eye contact with Kimberly. She recognized him and began to introduce him to David. "David…this is Dr. Gavarasana. He is the top brain surgeon at Memorial."

"How do you do," the doctor said with an Indian accent. "You must be the son."

"Yes, Doctor," David replied. "Brain surgeon? What is wrong with my mother?"

"We want to begin with a positron emission tomography," he began to reply, but was cut off by David.

"Wait a minute, Doc," David interrupted. "You will have to speak in plain English. You lost me—I have heard of MRIs and CAT scans."

"Much like MRI and CT scan," the doctor continued. "Except this procedure targets malignant tumor cells in the body."

"Tumor!" David said with shock. Kimberly squeezed his hand tightly.

"We will know soon," the doctor said as he glanced up at the clock. "I keep you informed."

The doctor exited quickly. Stunned, David sat down slowly on the sofa. Kimberly continued holding his hand. She comforted him in any way she could while trying to contain her own emotions. After a few minutes of silence, she noticed a change in his mood as he stared out in deep thought.

"What are you thinking?" she finally asked.

"Those migraines," he replied with anger in his voice. "I should have made her see a doctor a long time ago."

"Now you can't blame yourself for this," Kimberly quickly responded. "You could not have known anything about this... How long has she been having these migraines?"

"For years I think," he replied, as he looked into her eyes. "But they were worse the last few months."

An hour passed, which seemed like an eternity for David. Dr. Gavarasana entered the waiting room wearing scrubs, his mask dangled around his neck just below his chin, with perspiration soaked into the front edges of his cap. "Mister Paige," the doctor said. "It is confirmed. Craniopharyngioma tumor."

"Treatable?" David asked.

"Must have surgery now," he replied. "It is very big. Just above the pituitary gland. Possibly entwined with the optic nerves."

David bombarded the doctor with questions. "Will she survive? Can this be treated? Will she lose her sight?"

The doctor interrupted David's questions. "Mister Paige," he said, then hesitated so David could focus on what he had to say. "Risks in all surgeries. Many more in brain. Will not know how much, or can answer all your questions until I see inside." Then he paused. "Don't want to scare you. But don't want to sugar coat either. Fifty-fifty at this point. Maybe worse when inside… This be good time to pray."

David understood the doctor through his Indian accent and weak English. But he did not want to think about the possibilities. This was his mother. She had to pull through. David watched helplessly as the doctor walked away and disappeared through swinging doors. A cold chill overcame him, then Kimberly led him back to the sofa. Without a word, she stared into his lifeless eyes, then began to make phone calls on her cell to his boss and closest friends.

Four long hours later, David and Kimberly waited silently in the waiting room, accompanied by his boss, Alice's boss, a couple of deputies that David worked with, and two of his closest golfing buddies. David was restless and impatient because they had not gotten any word yet. Kimberly explained to him that these types of surgeries often took hours, sometimes all day. He rose and began to pace while constantly glancing over to the swinging doors the doctor had disappeared through. He imagined seeing the doctor walking briskly back through the swinging doors, taking off his sweaty mask, revealing a smile from ear to ear, then delivering wondrous news that they got it all and expected a full recovery. David smiled at these thoughts just as he turned around; then he froze as he saw Dr. Gavarasana making his way through the swinging doors. David's smile disappeared as he noticed that the doctor was not walking briskly but rather very slowly, as if wading through thick swampy water. His mask and most of his scrubs were soaked around the edges with perspiration and spackled with blood.

The doctor then slowly removed his mask, revealing not a smile but rather the face of a battle-scarred soldier. His tired eyes narrowed as he fixed them on David. He made his way directly to David without hesitation. His glassy eyes and the expression on his face told David that he had lost his mother.

Chapter 4

To David's surprise, the sun rose the next morning like every other day, as if this was a normal part of life. He could not comprehend this, because he felt heartbroken with a strange emptiness in the pit of his stomach. Kimberly stayed faithfully by his side all night, though neither could manage to sleep for any period of time. She knew exactly what he was going through. Kimberly had lost her father a few years back, the only man besides David that she adored.

Kimberly prepared him breakfast, but all he could do was play with it in his plate. By midday people began to roll in and out, bringing food as well as condolences. Neither comforted David in the least. He managed to put up a good front, greeting and thanking all who came by, some of whom he had never seen before— they must have been regulars at the library.

Around 2 p.m. he was forced by Kimberly to sit and eat. She gave him a couple of fried chicken wings and a glass of milk. He took a bite, but it seemed to grow bigger with each chew. As he attempted to wash it down with milk, he pictured his mom that last night sitting at the table with a glass of milk, the last time he saw her alive. Anger filled the void inside, overriding any appetite he had. He slammed the glass down and rushed out the back door. Behind the house was a tiny yard with the swing set still intact that he grew up on. He walked over to it as memories rushed through his mind. He drifted back as far as his memory would take him, feeling his mother push him on the swing as he laughed, increasing more the higher he flew. He rubbed his hand along the rusting chain and smiled, then tested the narrow seat as he eased his weight down on it. Realizing that it would not break, he began to swing just a bit. More memories rushed into David's mind, like angry waves rushing ashore. Alice was the only family he had, and he didn't know how he was going to move forward. He had taken for granted, as most all of us do, what it meant to have her in his life. And it had never dawned on him that she could be swept away so suddenly.

After about ten minutes, Kimberly ventured out the back door. She stopped when she spotted David on the swing and a relieved smile inched across her face.

"Just a few more minutes…please?" David asked.

Kimberly smiled then quietly returned to the guests inside. After ten minutes, as he said, David walked back inside. Kimberly was talking to a man in a three-piece suit he didn't recognize. He had gray hair slicked back with a thick mustache that made him very distinguished looking. Kimberly then noticed David and waved for him to come over. Reluctantly he walked slowly over to the two. When in reach, Kimberly took David by the arm. "David…this is Mr. Freeman."

David put on a fake smile. "Thank you for coming."

"He is the Funeral Director," Kimberly said very slowly.

David instantly felt trapped. He still had the man's hand in his, the very last person on this earth he wanted to see, much less talk to.

"I am sorry for your loss," Mr. Freeman said in a deep voice.

David retrieved his hand before it got the life squeezed out of it. "I am sorry, Mr. Freeman, I haven't had time to think about this."

"Everything is taken care of," he responded.

David's eyes narrowed a bit, and with confusion on his face he asked, "What, who?"

"May we speak in private?"

David led him into his bedroom, then shut the door behind them.

"Like I said," Mr. Freeman continued, "everything is taken care of. Alice came by five years ago. I believe you were in college." David nodded. "I showed her a couple of plots in the Magnolia Cemetery. And she fell instantly in love with them. The view over the water is breathtaking. She signed the deal right away, a plot for her and yours beside hers. Then she picked out a casket and planned her whole funeral."

"Okay, I understand," David responded. "A pre-planned funeral, that makes sense. So how much is left to be paid?"

"Nothing," he replied. "She paid in full that day."

This news confused David. His mother had pinched pennies all her life. "That must have cost a pretty penny."

"To the ring of twenty-four thousand dollars," Mr. Freeman responded.

"She must have put a lien on the house," David responded, for he was still confused.

"I don't think so," Mr. Freeman said. "I can remember that day like it was yesterday. Your mother was quite a negotiator. The actual total bill came out to twenty-four thousand six hundred and some change. She whipped out twenty-four thousand in one hundred dollar bills, and told me to take it or leave it. I had never seen that much cash before, so I took the money and ran."

David was overwhelmed. How did she have twenty-four thousand in cash? He thought to himself.

"You look as shocked as I looked that day," Mr. Freeman said.

"It is odd, I have to admit," David responded.

"That wasn't the only thing odd," he said. "I had to meet her that day before sunrise, nothing to do with the transaction. She wanted to see the view at sunrise. And it was a glorious one that morning. And I'm glad it was—that sealed the deal." He paused. "And leads to an odd request she has. Your mother requests her funeral to be at sunrise."

David nodded. "And that is what she will get."

"That's great," he responded. "I will get the programs printed and in your hands later this evening. The funeral will be at sunrise, Monday morning."

As soon as David thanked Mr. Freeman and bid him goodbye, he spotted Kimberly talking to another stranger in a suit. This man was shorter, about five and a half feet tall, with a very visible pot belly. He was wearing an ill-fitting grey pinstripe suit, with a blistering red tie adorned with a smiling Santa Claus. Kimberly spotted David and began to wave for him to come. David widened his eyes a bit while shaking his head slightly. She then gave him a look of distress, as if she needed to be rescued from this man in a Santa tie. The man turned his eyes upon David, forcing him to approach to keep from being rude.

"Darling," Kimberly said, stretching out the word as much as possible. "This is Mr. Chapman. He is your mother's attorney."

David shook his hand, as Kimberly disappeared. "I appreciate you coming by. I didn't realize that Mom had an attorney."

"Everyone should have a personal attorney of their own," Chapman remarked. "Don't you have one?"

"No...and I hope I won't need one anytime soon," David replied. "And I can't imagine my mother needing one."

"I know this is a bad time," Chapman said. "When would be a good time for you to settle your mother's estate?"

David stared into Mr. Chapman's brown eyes for a moment. "Oh yes...I am so sorry. The house, of course—please forgive me, my mind is not thinking straight. If all I have to do is sign some papers, then I can stop by your office one day this coming week."

Mr. Chapman began to have a confused look on his face. "It is not as simple as that."

David returned his stare, with the same confused look on his face.

"How about I come back in a few days," Chapman suggested. "Let's say Wednesday, the day before Thanksgiving, around 7 p.m. Maybe then you will be thinking much straighter. And again, I am sorry for your loss."

Mr. Chapman shook David's hand again and exited the house. Kimberly walked up slowly behind David. "Is it safe now?"

"Only until Wednesday," David replied. "He will be back around 7 p.m. I have to sign some papers putting the house in my name."

David turned his attention back to his guests, though he would much rather have crawled into a hole, away from people and away from reality. Kimberly stayed close, like a guardian angel, tending to his every need as best she could. They spent another restless night, neither getting much rest. The viewing was on Sunday afternoon. David hadn't shed many tears up to now, at least not publicly. The sight of his mother in the casket brought an uncontrollable rush of emotions, even though he admitted that she had never looked more beautiful. This was the first time he had ever seen her wearing makeup. When the viewing time had passed, he spent another twenty minutes alone with his mother for the last time.

The sun peeked over the horizon, a glorious view over the water, just like the morning Alice first saw it. A group of about thirty surrounded an open grave. An explosion of colors burst as sun rays met the multitude of flowers from the many friends. Kimberly and her best friend sang two of Alice's favorite songs. Then Alice's boss from the library got up and read an excerpt from her favorite book. The sun came into full view as the service ended, spewing out warmth on this cold occasion.

Chapter 5

David took the whole week of Thanksgiving off from work, he hoped to give him time to reflect and most of all time to heal. Unfortunately, he thought, Thanksgiving will forever be a bitter reminder of the loss of his mother. Mr. Chapman arrived on Wednesday as promised, passing through the white picket fence and knocking on the front door at seven sharp. David invited him in, steering him into the living room. He was wearing grey slacks with a navy blue blazer adorned with a different bright red Christmas tie. He was also carrying a black leather briefcase with golden latches. Kimberly entered the room, asking him if he wanted something to drink, which he declined graciously. She then took a seat close to David as Mr. Chapman opened his briefcase. "Now David," Chapman began, "you are the sole heir to your mother's estate."

David found the sound of his mother's estate very amusing. "Yes, I guess I'm the proud owner of this castle."

Kimberly poked him in his side, while Mr. Chapman raised an eyebrow at him.

"Yes indeed," Chapman said slowly. "The housing market is way down at this time. But this property is still valued at approximately $220,000." He rustled some papers. "Then there is her bank account. According to the will, she turns everything over to you at this point."

"A will?" David questioned as he looked to Kimberly. "I never knew she had a will."

"Of course she did," Chapman responded. "But being as there are no stipulations, it is all turned over to you. Therefore," he paused, "the total figure, which includes her checking and savings accounts, plus CDs and annuities, comes to a grand total"—he pecked on his calculator—"yes…two million, three hundred thirteen thousand dollars."

Silence filled the room. Mr. Chapman raised his eyes from the accounts, witnessing both David and Kimberly frozen in shock. "Is there something wrong with my calculations?" he asked, not aware that they didn't know.

David and Kimberly slowly turned towards each other, both reflecting the same expression.

"Are you sure about those figures?" David finally asked.

"Well, let me run them again." Mr. Chapman pecked on his calculator, like a child first learning to type. "Oops," Chapman said. "I made a slight boo boo."

"Slight," David said, and then he and Kimberly chuckled.

"Now I got it right," Chapman said. "I triple checked it this time. Okay, the grand total now is two million, three hundred thirteen thousand one hundred dollars."

David and Kimberly locked eyes once again. "What are you talking about?" David asked as he rose and took a seat next to Mr. Chapman.

"The figures are all right here," Chapman said as he handed David the copies of the bank accounts.

David scanned the papers, and then raised his puzzled face to stare at Kimberly. She rushed to the sofa and took a peek at the papers for herself.

"This is unbelievable," David remarked while looking at the figures.

"You had no idea of your mother's financial status?" Chapman asked.

"No sir," David replied. "Does this look like the home of a millionaire? Look in the driveway. Her car is ten years old."

"I don't know what to say," Chapman said. "Your mother was very good with investments and managing her fortune."

"Her fortune," David said in disbelief. "How? She worked at the library for God's sake."

"She volunteered her services at the library," Chapman responded. "She wouldn't take a penny. She just wanted to be around the books she loved. She had her fortune when she moved here in 1986."

"What!" David said, confused. "Moved? She didn't move here. This was her grandmother's house, the one who raised her. She passed away before I was born."

"Mr. Paige…David," Chapman said in a slow even tone. "I don't know what you have been told…but I have known your mother for twenty-five years, when she moved here in 1986. My wife was the real estate agent. She sold your mother this house on December 13, 1986. I can remember it clearly, because it was our first anniversary."

David sat back slowly, shaking his head and running his hands through his hair. "I'm sorry, Mr. Chapman. It's not that I think you are a liar, this is just the first I have heard about any of this. I just don't know what to think of it."

"I'm sorry," Chapman said. "I thought you knew. I was sworn to secrecy, and still am. Alice just wanted to live a normal life, and she did. You should be happy about that."

"You say she moved here in 1986?" David asked.

"Yes," Chapman replied. "You were just an infant…a preemie." He paused. "Wait a minute." He dug deep in his briefcase. "I forgot about the Trust Fund."

"Trust Fund!" David and Kimberly said simultaneously.

"Yes, here it is," Chapman said while pulling out an old document. "You also have a Trust Fund with Sovereign Bank in Philadelphia."

"And how much is that?" David asked.

"Two million dollars," Chapman replied, then hesitated. "At least that is what it was worth in 1986. It has probably tripled or better by now."

"Omigod!" Kimberly said, while flopping back in her seat.

"Yes Mr. Paige," Chapman said. "You are a very wealthy man."

David sat in silence, shocked at the money and the secrets. Mr. Chapman looked at David for a few moments, then turned to Kimberly. "I think he needs some time to digest all of this."

Kimberly nodded in agreement. Mr. Chapman pulled out an envelope, handing it to her. "Alice wanted David to have this. He can come by my office when he feels up to it. I just need a few signatures, legal stuff that's all." He closed the briefcase and shook Kimberly's hand.

"Thank you," she said, as she saw him out. Kimberly returned to the sofa, placing the envelope on the coffee table. She then sat close to David. "Are you okay?"

"Does any of this make sense to you? If so, please explain it to me," he said, frustrated. "And why did she keep it a secret? I just don't understand."

"Whatever the reason," Kimberly said, "it was definitely for the best."

"How so?"

"Well, just suppose she hadn't kept it a secret. And she had lived a rich lifestyle, with you included. Then you wouldn't be the person you are today," she explained. "Do you remember Richie Stevens in school?"

"You mean Richie Rich?"

"Yes," she replied. "That was a good nickname for him. His parents bought him everything he wanted. He was a spoiled brat. And where is he now?"

"In prison," he replied. "He got caught with a considerable amount of cocaine about a year and a half ago."

"That's right," she responded. "If he had been raised differently, then maybe he wouldn't be in prison now. Anyway, they always say, what you don't know won't hurt you. So what harm has come of this?"

David sat quietly, staring out into space, thinking. "I may have family out there somewhere."

"I guess it is possible," she said. "Could be in Philadelphia, which is where he said the Trust Fund is. She must have lived there before moving here."

"That makes sense."

"You can use your investigating skills to check it out, since you will have a lot of time on your hands. You are going to quit your job, aren't you?"

"Not right away," he replied. "I want to keep my inheritance a secret…please."

"Of course," she responded, then looked into his eyes. "You look exhausted. Let's get some rest."

He nodded as she took him by the hand, leading him towards the bedroom. She hit the lights as she went by. The bright moon shone through the window, illuminating the white envelope lying on the coffee table. David, caught by surprise from the secrets he learned that day, didn't realize that the biggest surprise was yet to come, from within the white envelope. The crimson key would prove to be the greatest mystery.

Chapter 6

Thanksgiving Day David and Kimberly finally got some rest, the first since Alice's death. David rose first at 9:30, made his way to the kitchen, then started a pot of coffee. The alluring aroma of freshly brewed coffee awakened Kimberly. Just as David was pouring his cup, she walked up close behind him and sighed. He grinned, knowing what she wanted, and surrendered his cup to her. They settled at the kitchen table.

"Happy Thanksgiving," she announced.

David grunted then took a sip of coffee. "The first," he said, then took another sip.

"First what?" she asked.

"The first Thanksgiving without Mom."

"Sorry…I wasn't thinking," she responded.

"No Kim," he said. "It's not your fault. I should have kept my thoughts to myself."

"No!" she demanded. "You have been doing too much of that as it is. I want you to let out your thoughts and feelings. It's not good to keep them bottled up inside. I know…remember, Dad died seven years ago today."

David jerked his head in her direction. Their eyes locked. "I am so sorry. I completely forgot."

She gave him a forgiving smile through glassy eyes. "That's okay…now we both will be counting Thanksgivings."

He leaned into her, kissing her gently on her lips. "Thank you."

"Why are you thanking me?" she asked.

David refilled her cup and returned the pot. "Thank you for everything you have done this past week. I don't know what I would have done without you. I should have thanked you before now…I have just been in another state of mind."

"It was my pleasure. You don't have to thank me."

"Oh yes I do," he responded. "You took care of everything…and me too."

She smiled at him, and then noticed him drifting off into thought. "You are supposed to let your thoughts and feelings out. No more bottling them up."

He blinked, as if awakening. "I just thought of something."

"I can see that…what is it?"

"I don't have any family at all, at least none that I know of." He took another sip of coffee. "I wonder if I have family in Philadelphia that I don't know."

"You might," Kimberly responded. "What did Alice tell you about your family?"

"She told me that she was an only child, like her grandmother and grandfather. Her mother died during labor. Her grandmother raised her here in this house. But now we know that is a lie. How much of it is true? Or is it all just one big lie? And why?"

Kimberly detected a hint of anger in his voice. "If Alice spared you from the truth, then she must have had a good reason. There is no need to get all worked up until you can see the whole picture. Will you have to go to Philadelphia to take care of your Trust Fund?"

"I guess I will," he replied. "Some time in the future."

"Why don't you take some time off? Then go to Philadelphia and maybe you can look up your family."

David rose, then went to the sink and rinsed out his cup as he gazed out the window. "That might be a good idea. I have enough time between vacation, comp time and sick leave to cover the rest of the year."

Kimberly rose while finishing her coffee. "Good… then you will do it?"

He hesitated, then took her cup and rinsed it out. "I don't know…probably not. I can take care of the Trust Fund through my bank here. If I decide to look up my family I will go to the internet."

Kimberly smiled while glancing at the clock. "Oh yes…you have been invited. Let me rephrase that, you were invited and you accepted."

David gave her a serious look. "And what did I accept this time?"

She gave him an innocent little smile. "Grandma is having Thanksgiving lunch at one p.m. She invited you." She paused. "And I kinda told her that you accepted."

David's stare gradually turned into a smile. "Well… since I have obligated myself, I guess I will have to go. A change of scenery may be good."

"My thoughts exactly," she responded.

They showered and dressed, then left shortly after noon. Meanwhile, undetected and forgotten by Kimberly, the envelope with the crimson key tucked away inside lay undisturbed on the coffee table. When David and Kimberly returned from her grandmother's, the lazy sun was just falling over the horizon. David made a straight line shot for the sofa. Flopping down, he gave a loud sigh. "Boy, I can't remember the last time I have eaten so much."

Kimberly chuckled. "Can I get you anything?"

"Definitely no food," he quickly replied. "But a Captain would be nice." He stretched out on the sofa, letting his food settle in his stomach. Just as he was getting into a comfortable position, the envelope caught his eye. He stared at it for a minute, then curiosity got the best of him. He sat up and plucked the envelope off the table just as Kimberly brought him his drink. "What is this?" he asked, as he felt the outside of the envelope.

"Oh, I forgot," she replied. "Mr. Chapman left that for you when he was leaving."

David shook the envelope and held it up to his ear. "There is something inside." He then ripped off one end of the envelope and poured out the contents into his other hand. Out fell a silver necklace with a crimson-colored key on the end. He held up the chain while staring curiously at the key.

"That is beautiful," Kimberly said as she took it out of his hand.

David watched her as she placed the necklace around her neck. Then he smiled as the crimson key disappeared within her cleavage. "Nice hiding place," he remarked.

Kimberly laughed as she pulled up on the chain, and the crimson key reappeared like magic. "This is too long for me," she remarked. "But it is beautiful. Is it Alice's?"

"I have never seen it before," he answered, then looked into the envelope. "There is a letter in here too." David pulled out the letter, instantly recognizing his mother's stationery. He took a large gulp of his Captain, then leaned back to read. "It's a letter from Mom."

"Could you please read it out loud?" Kimberly asked.

"Dear David, if you are reading this, then I must no longer be with you." David's eyes began to water. He wondered when she had written this. Could she have known in advance that she was dying and told no one? The thought angered him as he struggled to read on. "I want you to know that I could not have had a better child than you. And I hope that I have been the best possible mother to you. By now you must have many questions about the money." He nodded his head up and down. "I only wish that I was there with you to answer your questions. I was supposed to reveal the truth to you when you became an adult. But due to my selfish love for you, I could not, for fear of losing your love for me as your mother. Please forgive me. For this reason I have died a very happy mother, which would not have been possible if it were not for my sister's loving sacrifice. I pray that after you learn the truth, you will not love me any less." David looked up to Kimberly's puzzled face then dropped his eyes back to the letter. "Though I have loved you dearly as no other mother could have, I am not your biological mother."

David dropped his hand holding the letter, as he quickly stood. "What the hell?"

"Keep reading, keep reading," Kimberly insisted.

David paced slowly around the room as he continued to read. "Your biological mother is my twin sister, Amber."

"Omigod!" Kimberly blurted out.

David dropped a hand to his side, standing still with apparent shock on his face. Kimberly jumped up and took the letter from him as he slowly sat in the recliner nearby. Then she picked up where he left off. "She was a model for some firm in New York City. She came to me one night two days after you were born. She gave you to me because she feared for your life. Your father, whose name she would not reveal, threatened her if she did not abort. I have every reason to believe her because I saw a bruise on her cheek. It was a miracle that you were born early. He has no idea—he was under the impression that she had left to have an abortion. And he does not know that I exist."

David slowly rose, then returned to the sofa, taking a long swig of Captain Morgan. Kimberly watched him out of concern, then returned to the letter. "The affair was a threat to his marriage and his career. She still feared for her safety as well, but the only way to make sure that you would be safe was to give you to me. And she would return to New York City as if she had gone through with the abortion. She left me $4,000,000. I put half in a Trust Fund for you and relocated here where you would be safe. I have not seen or heard from her since. She also left me the crimson key to give to you. She said that if something bad happened to her, then the key would hold all the answers to her demise. Love forever, your mother Alice."

David finished off his drink, then took the glass to the kitchen for a refill. Kimberly sat on the sofa, reading silently back through the letter. "David, what are you going to do?"

"Fix me another drink," he replied. "A double this time."

"No…about this letter," she responded, and waited for a reply. The only sound that she heard was the clanking of ice cubes rattling inside his glass. She was still looking over the letter when he returned to the living room with a much larger glass of Captain Morgan in his right hand. He swept the crimson key off the coffee table as he took a big gulp of his drink. He stood, staring at the crimson key.

Kimberly raised her eyes, joining his stare. "I wonder what it fits in," she said, then raised her stare to David. "Are you okay? This has got to be a shock to you."

"A few more of these and I won't feel a thing," he remarked, then took another big gulp.

"Easy on the Captain," she said. "I might have to pay for that later."

He sat down once again, while Kimberly stared again at the letter. "What are you going to do about this?"

David waxed off the Captain Morgan, then sat the empty glass down hard on the table. The ice cubes clanked inside the empty glass. Kimberly slowly raised her head. "David!" she said loudly, then pointed at the empty glass. "Where did that go?"

He gave her a big smile. "AAARRRHH…down the hatch…mate," he replied in pirate talk.

"Omigod," she responded. "You have already set sail."

"Not yet, my dear…but I'm definitely feeling much better."

"Back to my question," she said. "What are you going to do about this letter? And that key?"

"I guess I have some investigation work to do."

"Does this mean you are going to Philadelphia?"

"Yep," he answered. "But there is no need to go until after this weekend. Everything will be closed up until Monday."

"Fly or drive?"

"I guess I will need to drive," he answered. "I will need a car to get around during my investigation."

"I have a suggestion," she said as she placed the key and the letter back into the envelope. "Your car has well over a hundred thousand miles on it. Why don't you take a little bit of your inheritance and buy you something more dependable."

"I will think about it," he said as he took his empty glass to the kitchen. "But right now I don't think I had better be driving."

Kimberly watched him glide into the kitchen. "AAARRRHH…You think so, mate."

Chapter 7

Monday afternoon, just a bit after 4 p.m., Kimberly walked out of Charleston Memorial. As soon as she passed through the automatic doors at the front entrance, her eyes latched on to a shiny new fiery red Camaro Z28 with tinted windows, parked innocently at the curb. As she approached from the rear, with her eyes still glued to the glossy fresh paint, the passenger side window slowly descended. Kimberly stopped, then reluctantly bent slightly to see who was inside. In the driver's seat sat David, wearing a grin from ear to ear. "Going my way?"

Kimberly's mouth dropped. "David!" she said loudly as she slid into the seat.

"You likey?"

"Me lovey," she replied, and then leaned into him and a kiss as well. "What possessed you?"

"You told me I needed something more dependable," he replied, then cranked the car, revving the powerful engine and pulling away from the curb.

"Where are you taking me?" Kimberly asked as she inspected the interior of the car.

"To dinner," he answered. "But first, before it gets dark, I want to get Mom's approval of the car."

Kimberly stared silently at him with a strange look on her own face. After a moment, and after he saw her reaction, he smiled. "I have fresh flowers in the trunk… they are for Mom."

She continued to stare at him, but her strange stare transformed into a smile. "I'm glad that you still refer to her as Mom." She took him by his hand. "I was afraid that you would be bitter."

"The initial shock made me bitter at first," he responded. "That is before the Captain sank in." David smiled. "No, seriously, she is the only mother that I have ever known. I still don't understand why she had to keep so many secrets, but like you said, she must have had good reason. Maybe it will all become clearer after the mystery is solved. I wish I could tell her somehow that I still love her dearly. And that this does not, and will never, change that, even if I find Amber."

"I think she already knows," she remarked. "So you will be searching for your other mother while you are in Philadelphia?"

"Yes," he replied, as he turned into the entrance of Magnolia Cemetery. "I took time off from work. And I got all my affairs straight with Mr. Chapman today."

Kimberly grew a worried look on her face. "The letter said that you were a threat to your father's career. You may still be in danger."

"I thought of that," he said, as he stopped the car and killed the engine. "During my investigation I will be using a false name, ID and credentials. Just like if I was working a real case. If someone gets suspicious and checks me out, it will be verified. Plus if a red flag pops up, my boss will inform me. I explained to him my situation and what I was going to do on my own time. He wants me to keep him in the loop."

"Me too!" she quickly responded.

"Of course," he said. "You are my partner in crime."

David and Kimberly placed fresh flowers around the fresh grave. Then they stood silently holding hands. The brilliant red sun drifted over the horizon, beaming a red reflection of light onto them and the water behind them, a picture perfect ending to this day.

David rose early the next morning, just before sunrise. Already packed, he headed west out of Charleston then north on I-95, eleven hours from his destination, Philadelphia. The farther from Mount Pleasant he drove, the less pleasant the weather became. By the time he reached Pennsylvania it was a frigid thirty degrees, with snow on the ground. He reached Philadelphia around 8 p.m., where he then checked in at a hotel, Hyatt at The Bellevue. After a nice ribeye steak and several Captain Morgans, he turned in for the night.

The next morning around ten, David entered the Sovereign Bank. He requested to see someone about his Trust Fund. Ten minutes passed, and then he was led into the office of Vice President Michaels, a tall thin man in his forties with thinning black hair and eyes to match. "Mr. Paige," Michaels said while shaking hands. "Please have a seat while I pull up your account. Did you bring proper identification?"

David handed him several pieces of identification, while admiring the spacious office with rich mahogany wooden furniture and desk to match. Then David's eyes landed on a large picture hanging on the wall behind Mr. Michaels. It was a picture of Mr. Michaels and Arnold Palmer in golfing attire. Mr. Michaels noticed David's stare. "You a golfer?"

"Yes sir," he replied. "It's a big sport where I come from."

"South Carolina," Michaels said with great expression, after reading David's ID. "I bet it is. Pretty nice weather year round, isn't it?"

"Very nice," David replied. "I have seen more snow today than I have in my entire lifetime."

Mr. Michaels laughed. "Well Mr. Paige…You can play a lot of golf with this Trust Fund. The net worth as of today is nine million, one hundred sixteen thousand."

"Wow," David responded.

"What would you like me to do with it?"

"Leave it be for now," David answered. "All I want today is some information. Is there a Philadelphia address on there somewhere?"

"Why yes it is," he replied. "Would you like for me to print this so you will have it for your records?"

"Please, and thank you."

Mr. Michaels smiled as he smacked a key on his keyboard, instantly starting a printer on a table against the wall. He then rose and walked to the printer the very second it finished printing. He retrieved the copy and promptly handed it to David. David looked over the paper for a few moments. "I see this was handled by a Mr. Mason. Is he still employed?"

"Yes he is," Michaels replied. "He is now the President of the bank. Would you like to speak with him?"

David nodded. "Please."

Mr. Michaels rang Mr. Mason. Shortly afterwards appeared a medium-size man pushing seventy, with snow white hair. David stood. "Mr. Mason?"

"Mr. Paige," the man replied with a handshake. "The last time I saw you, I could put you in the palm of my hand."

"I imagine so, from what I have heard," David responded. "Mom fed me real well since then."

"How is Alice?"

David's expression quickly saddened. "She passed twelve days ago, a brain tumor."

"Sorry to hear that," Mason responded. "Is there anything I can do?"

"I hope so," David replied. "Can you tell me anything about my family here?"

Mr. Mason thought a minute. "Your mom had a twin sister." He paused. "I believe her name was Amber. Very pretty as I recall. Last I heard she was a model in New York City."

"I know her mother died while in labor," David said. "What can you tell me about her grandparents?"

"The grandfather Elijah died in a railroad accident some years back. Catherine, the grandmother, raised the twins. Then she passed in 1985 I believe, cancer."

"Was there anyone else from the family?" David asked.

"Not that I know of, sorry."

David thanked them both and left.

After a nice lunch at a local bistro, David went to find the address from the bank records. He drove slowly down the street, reading the numbers on every house. Finally he reached the one he was searching for and came to a stop at the curb in front. He sat in his fiery red Z28, reminiscent of another one sitting in the very same spot, twenty-five years previous. Except this time he was in the driver's seat rather than in the passenger seat hidden inside a basket. A For Sale sign stared David in his face, a few feet from the curb. He slowly got out of the car, taking in all his surroundings, as if trying to trigger a long lost memory, impossible as it was since he was only days old at the time. He still looked around, trying to create a picture in his mind of a pair of twin girls playing in this street. He made his way to the house, then circled it while peeking in through dirty panes of glass.

"You looking to buy?" an old scratchy voice came from behind David.

Half startled, he turned to see an old man standing with a walker in his wrinkled hands, lurking near the Z28. David slowly approached him. "Right cold for you to be out and about, isn't it?"

The old man, wearing a dark green coat and pants to match, stared at David. "Cold?" he replied, scratching his head through his worn out Philadelphia Eagles stocking cap. Then he rendered a smile beneath thick plastic-rimmed glasses. "This ain't cold…you just wait until February."

"I imagine," David replied, as he stuffed his hands into his coat pockets. "You live around here?"

The old man slowly raised an arm, pointing a crooked shaking finger towards the second house down.

"My name is David Paige," he began to introduce himself, then was cut off by the old man.

"Paige," the old man repeated. "I remember Elijah Paige when he lived right here."

The old man probably couldn't remember what he had for supper the previous night, but his long term memory was as sharp as a tack. "He had one daughter," he rattled on. "But she died having babies…twins. The prettiest pair of little girls I have ever seen. Then Elijah was in an accident on the railroad. Catherine, now that was a good woman, she raised them two girls all by herself."

David listened patiently as the old man rambled on. Though prepared to ask him a few questions, he felt the need pass, for the old man was steadily spitting out David's family history.

"One of the girls…Amber I recall," he continued non-stop—"she was a pretty thing when she grew up. My wife Mary would get after me all the time, because I couldn't keep my eyes off her. Last I heard she moved off to New York City, a model of some kind. The other,

Alice, a year after Catherine passed away—cancer—had a baby out of nowhere. Then she suddenly disappeared. Elijah was an only child, and so too Catherine. You are the only other Paige I have ever heard of."

Then the old man jumped to another subject, continuously talking to himself as he slowly inched down the street, leaving David standing alone in the cold.

Chapter 8

David concluded that his search for Amber would have to continue in New York City. Every turn in Philadelphia led to more dead ends. The only information that he had to go on was that Amber worked for a modeling agency in New York City. Therefore she lived there at some point in time. His father was from New York City as well, or had strong business ties there. This career that he was worried about must be a high ranking position of some kind. This crimson key really had him puzzled, and it was supposed to provide all the answers. What did it go to? How did it fit into the equation? David informed his boss in Charleston that he would be heading to New York City the next day. He then made a call to his partner in crime, Kimberly. They talked for about an hour, and then he turned in.

When David woke the next morning, he stepped over to the window, opened the curtains, then looked out over Philadelphia. The sky was murky gray and lifeless, no sign of a sun. The uneven rooftops throughout the city looked like tree tops in a forest of pines, all snow-capped until spring. He tried to imagine living there, as his mother did twenty-five years ago. The cold winters must have been brutal, or was it something you just got used to and didn't think about? The white snow was beautiful, but he preferred white sandy beaches. After a good breakfast he checked out then headed to the city that never slept, New York City.

After several hours of horrific traffic, sometimes coming to a complete stop, David was ready to park and ride the subway instead of dealing with this headache. He found the parking garage he had located on the internet and then paid for a week in advance. He hopped a cab to Manhattan, Hilton New York, near the center of the metropolis. After checking in, David grabbed a late lunch, just after 2 p.m. A pizza lover, he decided to try some famous New York Style pizza, since he had heard so much about it. He enjoyed its unique flavor.

He then headed to the headquarters of the New York Police Department located at One Police Plaza in lower Manhattan. Upon arrival, he was directed to Detective Ricardo Moreno, a shorter than average man with a roll of fat around his midsection similar to a wooden barrel. He had a thick black mustache with dark black hair around the edges of his balding head. He led David to a much unorganized desk. Besides a computer screen and keyboard, the rest of the desk was cluttered with papers of all kinds, even a burger wrapper from lunch.

"Have a seat," Moreno said. "Excuse the mess. I'm going to have to fire the housekeeper." He then let out a big laugh.

David only grinned, as he thought to himself that Moreno probably used that line every day. "Mr. Moreno…my name is David Paige. I am a detective from the Charleston County Sheriff's Department."

"Nice to meet you," Moreno responded as he scratched his thick mustache. "Stay right here—I'll be right back."

David watched him walk briskly away, his rolls of fat bouncing as he walked. His pants, too long for his five-foot-five frame, were gathered on top of his dirty black leather shoes. After a few minutes he returned, carrying a small bag and two cups. The top of his polished bald head reflected from the lights overhead. He sat and handed David a cup and the small bag. "Help yourself," Moreno said. "We must keep up our strength."

David peered curiously into the bag, spotting four Krispy Kreme doughnuts. "No thank you…I had a late lunch. But thanks for the coffee."

"Okay," Moreno responded, stretching out the word. "That just leaves more for me."

David took a sip of the hot coffee. "I am looking for someone."

"Ahhh," Moreno sighed. "We spend ninety percent of our time looking for people, don't we?"

"Probably so," David remarked. "I am looking for my mother."

Moreno's eyes popped wide open, and he swallowed his half-chewed doughnut. He sat up straight in his chair, suddenly getting very serious. With a tap of his finger, he woke up the computer screen. "Well then," Moreno said as he stared at the screen while punching keys. "When was the last time you seen your mother?"

"Never," David answered.

Moreno froze. Then with a puzzled look on his face, he slowly turned to David. "Would you like to start from the beginning?"

"It's a long story," David replied. "To sum it up, my biological mother gave me away to her sister when I was an infant. My mother—who is really my aunt—moved from Philadelphia to near Charleston, South Carolina. She passed away just before Thanksgiving… my mother…who is really my aunt but is the only mother I have ever known."

Moreno leaned back in his chair. "This sounds like a soap opera. We got to take this slowly. You lost me at the mother aunt, but really mother part. You mentioned Philadelphia in there somewhere. How does New York City play into the picture?"

"My biological mother was a model in New York City at that time," David replied.

"Now we are getting somewhere," Moreno remarked, turning back to the computer screen while cramming half of a doughnut into his mouth. "Do you think she is still here?" he asked, spitting out small pieces of doughnut in the process. He then blew the crumbs off the keyboard.

"I'm not really sure that she is even alive," David replied. "No one has seen or heard from her since that night twenty-five years ago."

"I see," Moreno remarked. "What do you know about your mother?" He grabbed a pen and pad to take notes.

"Her name is Amber Paige," David said while Moreno scribbled. "She worked for a modeling agency in New York City. After leaving me with her twin sister in Philadelphia, she returned to New York City. That was November 15, 1986…and she was never heard from since."

Moreno inhaled another doughnut and sat back in his chair. "That's not much to go on."

"Yes I know," David said. "I thought we might check the missing persons file first."

"Did anyone ever report her missing?"

"No idea."

"What do you know about your father?" Moreno asked.

"Even less," David replied. "I don't even have a name. All I know is that he hit her and threatened her if she didn't abort the pregnancy. I was a threat to his career."

"Sounds like an affair," Moreno remarked. "And he was in some type of powerful position." He gave David a serious stare. "You may still be a threat to his career or marriage…that is if he is still alive."

"Yes…I know."

Moreno glanced at the clock. "Are you on the clock?"

"No," David answered. "I am doing this on my own time. And for once in my life, I don't have to punch a clock."

"That must be nice," Moreno remarked, while his eyes were glued to the clock. "My clock will need punching in fifteen minutes. I want to help you… Can you meet me here at 9 a.m.?"

"No problem," David replied. "And I will bring doughnuts."

Moreno shined a great big smile. "I knew I liked you the first time I saw you."

Both rose and exchanged business cards. Moreno stared peculiarly at David's card. "David Peoples?"

"Oh yes," David responded. "I will be under cover while I'm here. Just in case I am still a threat."

"That's a good idea," Moreno remarked as he walked David out.

"I'm staying at the Hilton New York," David said. "By the way…where is a good place to go for a drink?"

"Do you like hip or swanky?"

"I'm just looking for a drink," David said. "I'm not looking for anything else."

"Hey, this is New York," Moreno said with expression. "You don't have to be looking for anything …in New York, it usually finds you."

They both laughed out loud.

"Try the Tenjune," Moreno said. "In New York… you can't go wrong no matter which way you go."

They both laughed again.

Chapter 9

At the suggestion from the clerk at the front desk of the hotel, David treated himself to some of the finest Chinese food he had ever put into his mouth. Afterwards, he hailed a cab and headed towards the meat packing district to one of New York City's hottest nightclubs, the Tenjune. Once there, he fell into a line of hopeful attendees. It reminded him of the long lines at the amusement park. In the front of the line stood four gigantic bouncers, two near the entrance and two standing close to a tall thin well-dressed man. The two bouncers stuck with the tall man as he sifted through the line, handpicking certain lucky ones to enter the club. Luck really had nothing to do with it—good looks or money or both got them in. Though the man choosing didn't know David had plenty of money, he fortunately chose him on his good looks alone. David entered and descended into the subterranean club. It was jam-packed, the music deafening.

David watched people dance on the crowded horseshoe-shaped dance floor underneath disco and strobe lights. The décor of the room had a unique blend of wavy wood grains, accented in marble. He shuffled his way through the immense crowd until he reached a beautiful leather-clad bar. To his surprise, a stool was unattended. He first looked around then quickly hopped aboard. A very young, barely legal bartender came to his aid. David ordered a Captain Morgan and Coke, and then turned to watch the people dance as a DJ spun a mixture of the top pop and hip hop songs.

Though everyone there was attractive due to the hand-picking outside, David's eyes latched on to one particularly beautiful lady. She appeared to be in her middle twenties, about five foot nine with light ash brown hair. Her slender body fit snugly into the satin blue cowl neck cocktail dress that she wore so nicely. For some odd reason, David could not break his eyes away from her, drinking in her beauty. Then as if she sensed his attraction to her, she looked towards him while dancing. Their eyes connected, drawing a smile from David's face. The connection was suddenly broken as she spun around in dance. His eyes followed her as she spun in and out of the dancers on the crowded floor. Then as she came closer their eyes connected again, as if a magnet drew them together, and she returned his smile. Just as he began to smile back, the crowd swallowed her once again. David stretched his neck like a giraffe, trying to catch another glimpse of her. Temporarily surrendering to the crowd, he turned his attention back to his Captain Morgan.

"Another?" the bartender asked, noticing his glass nearly empty.

"Not quite yet," David replied, while wondering who this beautiful woman was. Then he remembered what he had told Detective Moreno—that he was looking only for a drink, nothing else. As he sat in heavy thought, the bartender slid him a fresh Captain and Coke. David looked up. "I thought I said not quite yet."

The bartender smiled while pointing. "Compliments of the babe in blue."

David turned in the direction of his pointing. The babe in blue turned out to be the beautiful lady he had shared stares with. Then he remembered what else Moreno had said—you don't have to be looking for anything…in New York it usually finds you. She now sat in a tiered plush seat, along with two other women, at the other side of the Club. She smiled at him while holding up a martini glass. He returned her smile, then turned quickly to retrieve his complimentary drink to hold up to her in thanks. When his eyes returned, she had disappeared once again. His eyes searched the room over, but there was no sign of her anywhere. Disappointed, he returned to his drink.

After a few minutes, the bartender approached him again. "Are you married or gay?"

David almost choked at the question. "What!"

The bartender shook his head at him. "You have to be either married or gay."

"Neither," David responded. "Why do you think that?"

"A beautiful woman buys you a drink…and you just sit there."

"It's complicated," David responded, taking a long sip.

The bartender dried a glass. "Where is she at?"

David sat his drink down. "Who?"

"The complication you are referring to."

"Oh," David responded. "Back home in South Carolina."

The bartender smiled. "What happens in New York City…stays in New York City…if you are careful."

David smiled through ice cubes as he turned up his drink. After ordering another, he turned around, spotting the lady in blue. "Fix me one of those," David demanded while pointing.

The bartender nodded, then quickly mixed a martini. David paid, then maneuvered carefully through the crowd, trying not to spill a drop from either drink. Finally he completed his mission and stood face to face with the beautiful lady in blue. She greeted him with a warm smile.

"Thank you," she said as she took the drink, moving it directly to her lips. She turned the drink up, draining about half of it, when suddenly her eyes popped wide open as the DJ began a very popular tune. Without introductions, she grabbed his hand and pulled him out onto the crowded dance floor—his first time dancing since his college days. David thoroughly enjoyed it, all the more so with such a beautiful partner. Their eyes locked constantly as they spun and swirled. The satin blue of her cocktail dress drew out the intense blue in her eyes.

After forty-five minutes of nonstop action, she finally led him away from the dance floor, reuniting with their drinks. Without a word, she drained the rest of the martini and then picked up a small shiny purse. David watched her motions as she walked away towards the ladies room. Aware of his stare, she quickly turned her head, catching him in the act. She rendered a smile as she disappeared through the door.

David took a thirsty gulp of his watered-down drink and checked his watch, 10 p.m. He smiled at the other two ladies, as they were looking him over. After watching the dancing for a while, he checked his watch again, 10:20 p.m. When he looked up he noticed the two friends had disappeared as well. He spent the next half hour searching the Club and then, disappointed, left and returned to his hotel room.

Chapter 10

David stopped by a nearby bakery the next morning, purchasing an assortment of fresh doughnuts. He entered the Police Department at precisely 9 a.m., not a second after. Detective Moreno met him at the door, two cups of coffee in hand. "Punctual…I like that… armed with pastries…even better."

They both chuckled as they made their way to Moreno's desk. Catching David by surprise, the desk was clean, not a paper anywhere, just a computer screen and keyboard resting on top of a handsome mahogany desktop. "I see you fired the housekeeper."

Moreno laughed. "Haven't been here long enough to destroy it yet." He then took a doughnut hostage. "Ahhh…fresh doughnuts…you are my hero." He crammed a white powdered doughnut into his mouth, filling his thick mustache with white powdered sugar, giving the appearance of fresh fallen snow in a dense forest. "We have a slight dilemma."

David took a long sip of hot coffee. "And what might that be?"

"Our missing persons file in the computer only goes back twenty years. Any reports before that time will be stored in the Dungeon, as we call it…the basement."

David finished his cup of coffee. "I hope you have had enough doughnuts to keep your energy up. Because it looks like we have some grunt work to do."

Moreno put his computer screen to sleep. "We'll take the rest of the doughnuts…just in case I begin to feel weak."

They both laughed. He took David to the Dungeon, which was not a fitting name for this basement. A more appropriate name would be the Jungle, because it was unorganized beyond recognition. Moreno cursed every five minutes, finding something out of place or missing.

David could not understand why Moreno was so irate—he should be used to messes by now, after the apparent condition of his desk the day before. "Make sure you fire the housekeeper down here too."

Moreno continued to mumble, cursing under his breath. "I know of a few officers who need to be strung up under an old oak tree. Then buried in this mess they created."

David smiled, but Moreno seemed serious. "How is your strength holding up?"

Moreno looked at his watch. "I have been so pissed off—I mean busy—that I completely forgot about my stomach."

"That might be a sure fire way for you to lose some weight. Just leave you down here for a while and watch the pounds melt away."

Moreno didn't laugh. "We might be down here a few weeks as it is."

David glanced at his watch, as his own stomach began to roar. "I think you need a break. I will spring for lunch."

At the sound of the word lunch, life suddenly returned to Moreno's face. "You like Italian?" David shrugged. "I'll take you to the best Italian restaurant this side of Italy."

"Is it fattening?"

Moreno patted his belly, like petting a dog. "I eat there all the time."

"Guess that answers my question."

They both laughed again. Two hours later, David paid the check and had to admit that Moreno might have been right. That was the best Italian food he had ever eaten. "Aren't you going to get in trouble for taking a two-hour lunch?"

Moreno worked a toothpick with precision inside his mouth. "We are working."

"We are?"

"Yes, of course…all I have to do is say that we went to see Mike Scully about your case. Scully has… ugh, I mean, will vouch for me. He doesn't like my boss anyway."

David smiled at the slip up. "Who is this Mike Scully?"

"Ahhh…Scully was the man in his day, memory like an elephant. Especially a face, he would never forget a face. Never forgot a name either. He retired ten years ago, not by choice. He would have worked until he croaked if they would have let him."

"Do you think he would remember my mom's case?"

"It wouldn't surprise me…if she was actually reported missing. He doesn't live far from here. It can't hurt…plus I need a good alibi."

Moreno took David to Brooklyn Heights, a culturally diverse neighborhood within the New York City borough of Brooklyn. They entered a street lined with a crowded row of houses, packed side by side like a row of sardines in a can. They approached a particular building of old brick and mortar, once completely painted over in a rustic red brick shade with a flight of ten steps that led up to a pair of flat gray doors beneath a rounded archway.

Moreno rapped on the door, and then sounds of footsteps drew closer from within. The door squeaked open, revealing a frail man who looked to be in his eighties. "I be damn," said the old man with a smile that filled his face. "Moreno…how the hell are you?"

The two men hugged. "Just getting by…it hasn't been the same without you." Moreno turned to David. "Scully…I'd like you to meet David Paige."

David shook his bony hand while throwing a surprised eye at Moreno.

"Oh," Moreno responded to the look. "My bad…but it's okay. Scully is like family. You can trust him."

Scully led the two into an informal living room, neat and tidy, opposite of Moreno's work area. They came to rest on a Victorian sofa with a large window at their backs. The old wooden floor was smothered by a Persian rug, with rich reds and golds that accented the burgundy upholstery of the Victorian sofa. Sitting elegantly in front of the sofa was an antique Barclay Square coffee table, its burnished cherry brownstone finish with rustic cherry veneers rested on legs of intricate detail. The room had a hint of cigar smoke lingering throughout.

Scully sat in a black leather recliner, not fitting with the rest of the décor. He held a crooked finger on his gray mustache, with a look on his face as if in deep thought. "Paige," he said slowly, stretching the word. "That name rings a bell."

Moreno poked David. "See…I told you…the man has the sharpest memory of anyone I know."

"I hope that is true," David said. "I was hoping you could help me. Amber Paige, my biological mother, went missing in 1986. We don't even know for sure that a missing person report was filed. We haven't seen any evidence of it in the Dungeon."

"I don't have the memory Moreno claims I do," Scully replied, his pale blue eyes matching the sweater he wore. "I have to keep notes. And I have kept notes on every case I have ever worked on. They are in the filing cabinet. But I don't need notes for this case. I remember this case in particular. Amber Paige," he repeated the word slowly, as if the name haunted him. "She was a beautiful lady. Yes, her roommate did file a missing person report. Then she came up missing three days later—her sister filed that report. Neither one was ever found."

"So the case is still open?" David asked enthusiastically.

"No," Scully quickly replied. "That is why I remember it so well. I almost lost my job because of it, due to insubordination. I argued with my boss over closing the case."

"So why did he close it?"

"Two reasons, which only led to speculations, not based on evidence. Being a model, or should I say a full-time paying model, is a difficult profession for many young women. It's a well-known fact that some supplement their income through dating services, if you know what I mean. Thus was the case with your mother's roommate, but not your mother. Or at least there wasn't any substantial evidence to prove it. But my boss implied that your mother did the same, since they were roommates. His speculation strengthened when we found evidence that your mother was pregnant. Most of the clients with these dating services are very rich or powerful. So my boss took the easy way out."

David rose, then walked to the window, staring through the frosted panes, as he controlled his anger. "May I look at the notes you have on my mother's case?"

Scully agreed without hesitation, leaving the room then bringing back his notes inside a manila folder. David made his own notes from Scully's, taking down the name of the modeling agency, her roommate's name, and the name of her roommate's sister from Albany, New York. After a few more minutes of Moreno and

Scully trading war stories, they all headed to the front door. Upon opening the door, frigid air rushed at them, biting the bare skin left unprotected.

David stopped. "One more question if I may?"

Scully closed the door partially, blocking the bitter wind, and he nodded.

"Were you working with a partner on this case?"

Scully nodded. "Yes…a snotty-nosed rookie…his name was Pete Sullivan."

Chapter 11

Moreno and David made it back to the police headquarters twenty minutes before the end of his shift. They returned to Moreno's untouched desk. "The cleaning lady sure will be in for a surprise tonight," David said.

Moreno stared at his desk for a moment. "That just doesn't look right," he said, and he opened a drawer, spraying papers all over the desktop. "There…she will feel right at home."

They both caught a laugh. David noticed movement out of the corner of his eye. From Moreno's desk, he had a clear view up the main aisle to the entrance. He turned his head towards the movement. A small group—two men in police uniforms, two men in expensive suits, and one familiar face—walked steadily from the other end of the department. The familiar face was the lady in blue from the nightclub. David quickly stood as the entourage made the turn towards the entrance. He stared with eyes and soul. Her eyes suddenly revolved in his direction, as if drawn by a magnet. She came to an abrupt stop, the others leaving her standing. Their eyes fixed upon one another as they stood center aisle, fifty feet apart, like two gunfighters waiting for the other to make the first move.

David made the first move. Frozen, he could only render a smile. Then, in her modern sleek heather grey blazer, pencil skirt to match, and glossy black Trotters, she made the next move, returning his smile. Her eyes twinkled as she turned and continued towards the door. Still frozen, David gazed to where she once stood, reminiscing of the night before dancing at the Club.

Moreno broke David's gaze. "Hey lover boy…I am afraid you can't afford that sweet honey."

David stretched his neck, trying to catch another glimpse. "Who is she?"

"Sheridan Blakely," Moreno answered, pronouncing the last name louder as if it had importance. "Blakely," he repeated again. "Mean anything?"

David turned in disappointment and took a seat. "Sorry, doesn't ring a bell."

"As in Senator Robert Blakely."

David shook his head and shrugged. "Not into politics."

"Sheridan Blakely—she is the daughter, only child of Senator Robert Blakely. She is fresh out of law school, quickly making a name for herself with the top law firm in Manhattan. They all were coming from the interrogation room. She looked at you like she knew you."

David took another look to the entrance, hoping she had returned. "I danced with her at the Tenjune last night."

"I thought you were only looking for a drink, not anything else?"

David smiled. "You did say you don't have to be looking for anything in New York…it usually finds you."

They both laughed out loud. About that time a thick broad-shouldered, medium-height, middle-aged man passed Moreno's desk. "Hey Sullivan," Moreno called out.

The man stopped, hesitating as if he didn't want to acknowledge Moreno. He slowly turned around. With an angry disposition, he responded. "What do you want?"

Moreno stood. "I want you to meet David Peoples… private eye."

David stood, sticking out a hand. Sullivan scowled at David with dark eyes, then glared at his outstretched hand. "I understand you used to be Mike Scully's partner," David said, still waiting for a handshake.

Sullivan's dark eyebrows rose at the sound of Scully's name. He surrendered his hand to David. "You are a private investigator?"

David released Sullivan's broad thick hand. "Yes sir, I am investigating a missing person case that you and Mr. Scully worked twenty-five years ago…Amber Paige."

Sullivan stared at David as if trying to read him, forever burning the image of David's face into his mind. "That was a long time ago. I don't remember that name," he lied. "Twenty-five years ago, you say."

"Yes sir, Amber Paige…a model."

"I have had many cases in the last twenty-five years. Who hired you? You got a card?" Sullivan took a card from David, staring at the name, David Peoples.

"The person who hired me wants to remain anonymous. If you recall anything, would you please give me a call?"

Sullivan continued to stare at the card. "Yeah, sure… you checked the database?"

"Had to search the Dungeon," David replied. "Haven't run across anything yet—just got started."

"That's right, Pete," Moreno said. "Cases over twenty years and you have to search the Dungeon. When was the last time you been down there?" Moreno asked in an insinuating manner.

"Good luck," Sullivan said, walking away in a hurry.

"Never liked that bum," Moreno said while scowling at Sullivan as he left. "I just don't trust that SOB."

David turned back to Moreno. "Guess we're done for the day."

"Weekend too, I hope."

"Yes…I guess we can put it on hold until Monday," David responded, drifting off in thought.

Moreno took notice of his mindless gaze. "You have anything planned?" he asked, saying the word anything much louder than the others.

David grinned, knowing what anything he was referring to. "Not really…but this is New York… anything may happen."

They both laughed. David headed for the entrance. When passing the reception desk, an officer spoke out,

"Mr. Peoples." David continued, not recognizing right away his undercover name. "David Peoples!" the officer said, nearly shouting.

David stopped abruptly at the door, then turned and walked back to the desk.

"There is a note left here for you," the officer said, handing David the note.

"Thank you," David said. His curiosity easily overtook him, especially since the note was on a folded pink piece of paper. He opened it quickly, not caring who might see it.

The note read: I wish to dance with you tonight, Tenjune. Leave your name at the door. They will be expecting you.

Just below the last word, a smiley face was drawn, instead of revealing her name. David smiled just as his phone began to vibrate, an unexpected call from Kimberly. He answered before leaving headquarters. After about twenty minutes of filling her in, he hung up, then exited and hailed a cab. Unaware of being watched, David entered the cab, gave the driver his destination—Hilton New York—then sat back, thinking only of the night to come.

Chapter 12

Pete Sullivan watched intently as a cab pulled away from the curb at headquarters with David inside. Once the cab was well out of sight, and knowing that Moreno had long gone, he opened his cell phone.

Not too far away, a white limousine cruised down Henry Hudson Parkway, through Washington Heights, just past I-95. A Blackberry danced in the rear seat. "Hello," a man in a deep voice answered.

"I have some information you would be interested in," Sullivan said.

The man in the limo hesitated, and then closed the window to the driver. "I told you not to call me anymore."

"Amber Paige," Sullivan said slowly, then hesitated a long while. "Am I on the payroll?"

The man in the limo clinched his fist. "What have you got?"

"How much?"

The man in the limo hesitated again. "You had better not be jerking my chain," he said in a low angry voice.

"Have I ever?" Sullivan asked, then paused. "It has been a long time, the cost of living has tripled."

"I'll double it…not a damn bit more!"

"Deal," Sullivan responded. "There is a private detective here looking into the Amber Paige case."

"Do you know him?"

"No," Sullivan replied. "Out of towner, I think. Got a small Southern drawl. I will check him out."

"You did take care of the records, didn't you?"

"Years ago, they were destroyed," Sullivan answered. "And the case is nowhere in the database."

"Then what's the problem?"

"Mike Scully," Sullivan replied. "I think Moreno told him that we worked the case together."

There was a long pause. "I told you we should have taken care of this back then," the man in the limo said. "But you didn't want to tie up all the loose ends."

"It was too risky then," Sullivan responded. "There were no relatives, and no one inquiring about her. It was so easy."

"It's not so easy now…is it?"

"Easier now," Sullivan replied. "As far as Scully goes—I can take care of him and his notes. But I'm not sure about this private eye…or who hired him."

There was silence for a minute. "Take care of Scully before they talk to him," the man in the limo instructed. "Check out this private dick. Email me any pertinent information you find. Find out who hired him. I don't care how you do it, just cover your tracks. You can't kill him until we find out who hired him."

"I will take care of Scully this weekend. I overheard Moreno say they were picking back up on the case Monday. That will give me time to check out the dick as well."

David arrived at Tenjune only to find a line twice as long as the night before. Luckily tonight he would not have to wait in line hoping to be picked, for he had a special invitation. Just as he exited the cab, a BMW Roadster Z4 swerved to the curb with a sudden stop. The beauty caught David's eye with its deep sea blue metallic paint and chrome spoke wheels. David spotted the New York license plate: SHERIDAN. His anticipation rose as he saw her rise from within the roadster, dressed in a white long ruffle trim dress that crossed over in the front. A silver shawl across her shoulders was all that protected her from the frigid air. The sexy firm-fitting dress left very little for the imagination. She was adorned with dangling diamond earrings that sparkled like the stars. Her glistening silver high heel shoes brought her up close to David's height.

Not noticing David amidst the crowd, she shot straight in under the protection of the bouncers. David waved at her, but her unwavering eyes were focused straight ahead for the door. He maneuvered around the crowd just as Sheridan entered. "I am with her!" he shouted at the bouncer, pointing to Sheridan.

Sheridan stopped at the sound. From just inside, but not out of sight, she made eye contact with the bouncer. With a smile and nod of her head, David was released to enter. David followed Sheridan closely inside, hand in hand, to a table reserved in her name. The club was already crowded, and the DJ had them all in motion. David removed her shawl while planting a tender kiss on her cheek. "What does the lady wish to drink?" he asked.

"Why David," she said, giving him a smile, for his politeness pleased her, "you are a true Southern gentleman."

"How did you know my name? And how do you know I'm from the South...Sheridan?"

She gave him another smile then leaned in close to him. "First of all, I'm a lawyer...I have my ways of finding out what I want to know. The second is easy...I detect a slight Southern sexy drawl in your voice." She laughed. "So how do you know my name?"

David laughed. "I too have my ways...I'm a private detective, and I will not reveal my source."

She leaned in close again. "Mine was easy...my name is on my license plate."

"Very true, my dear," he admitted. "But there wasn't enough room to put Blakely on the plate."

Her eyes and mouth popped open. "You are very good. Now what drink do I want?"

David remembered the drink from last night. "I believe you would like a martini."

"Not bad...but what kind?"

David laughed while shutting his eyes and shaking his head.

"That's okay darling," she said up close. "I will give you an A for effort. It's an apple martini…and don't forget to order your Captain Morgan and Coke."

David shook his head in defeat, while laughing as she laughed in triumph. After only one sip of his drink, she dragged him willingly to the dance floor. They danced for hours, connecting in many ways, strangely for no longer than they had known each other. David tired, while she didn't seem to, relentlessly moving her slender body all over the dance floor. David glanced at his watch, 1 a.m. "Do you ever quit?"

"Never!" she shouted, then laughed. "This is my workout. I don't run or exercise to stay in shape…this is my workout. I dance at least four times a week. Good for my body and good for my mind. Plus it keeps me away from home…and Dad."

David sensed the resentment when she mentioned her father; her face suddenly saddened. "But I do need to call it a night…got plans tomorrow."

David paid the tab and they exited, bodies touching as they walked. "Can I drop you off somewhere?" she asked.

"I don't want to put you to any trouble."

"Nonsense," she responded, as they brought her roadster to the curb.

"That is one gorgeous machine," David said, his eyes finally on something besides Sheridan.

"Why thank you," she responded, tossing him the keys. "You drive…I have got to take my shoes off. These heels are killing me."

David opened the door for her and then crawled into the driver's side of the small sports car.

"Where are you staying?" she asked, slipping out of her heels.

"Hilton New York."

"Nice," she said, stretching out the word. "I will show you the way."

While driving, David reached over, brushing her cheek with his fingers. "Thanks for the invitation. I had a wonderful time… I'm not sure how long I will be in New York City, but I would like to see you again. We didn't get much time to talk…to get to really know one another."

She didn't answer, just smiled at him. He was not sure what to say now. He thought he had said too much as it was. What would a beautiful rich lady want with him? All she knew was that he was a private eye from the South. He noticed she was thinking hard about something, and she looked like she was about to say something, but she didn't.

"Let's get one thing straight," she finally said, pointing a finger as if scolding him. "We don't know each other at all." She paused, while he sat stunned. "But," her voice mellowed out, "there is something about you…I can't explain it, but I really want to get to know you better." She paused again. "I don't want you to get the wrong impression—I don't do this. And don't get your hopes up. I am not promising anything."

David was really confused at this point but was afraid to ask what she meant. Instead he said the most logical thing he could think of: "Okay." He said it very slowly, so if it was not the right thing he could flow into something else. He detected that it must have been a good answer, because she didn't jump at him. Then again, he was not sure because she got quiet. She then stared at him quietly while he drove.

After a few minutes, which to him seemed like an eternity, she rendered that same smile he remembered. "My father owns a home in the Catskill Mountains," she said, then paused. "When he is here at home, I usually go up there for the weekend."

He sensed that resentment again.

"Would you like to spend the weekend with me up there?" she asked sweetly.

David's eyes popped open in shock. Then that finger shot up again before he could reply. "I don't do this— don't judge me. And I told you not to expect anything or get your hopes up."

"I would love to," David replied in an even mild tone. "And don't forget…I'm a Southern gentleman."

She smiled. "I will pick you up at 8 a.m."

Chapter 13

David walked out of the Hilton New York at precisely 8 a.m., not a second later, punctual as always. The sky was an even murky gray color, with a bitter cold breeze that stung his cheeks. A steady snow fell, a light fluffy snow that danced about, blanketing the ground about an inch. David searched for a BMW Roadster, but all he could see was a snow white Hummer SUV, with two pairs of snow skis tied down on the roof rack. He checked his watch just as a horn tooted. In the direction of the sharp toot sat only the Hummer. He instantly noticed the plates: BLAKELY.

David smiled then recognized a familiar smile through the frosted windshield. He made his way to the Hummer, taking notice that it was entirely encased in chrome, including the wheels. He opened the rear door, depositing his luggage, and then climbed aboard on the passenger side. Sheridan gladly greeted him with a quick kiss on the lips. "Good morning."

"Good morning to you," David responded. "I sure am glad to see you driving this."

Sheridan smiled. "You weren't expecting my little Beemer, were you?"

He shrugged. "I wasn't sure." He looked around inside. "Nice toy you got here."

Sheridan's smile faded quickly. "It's my father's."

David sensed the resentment at the mention of her father, the same resentment he had noticed before. Attempting to change the subject, and hopefully her mood to match, he pointed at the end of the snow skis protruding just into view over the top of the windshield. "Is that snow skis?"

Her smile returned. "Oh yes…the house is only a five-minute drive from Belleayre Mountain." She paused. "New York's winter snow park."

David had an almost frightened look on his face. "I have never skied before."

Her smile widened even more. "I was hoping you haven't…I will teach you, and I promise you will love it."

David stared out the side window at some cars that had already slipped off the slick road. "How long a drive is it?"

"About a three-hour drive…maybe a little more today."

"That's good," he remarked, while turning slightly in his seat in her direction.

Sheridan watched out the corner of her eye as he got situated. "Why is that?"

"It will give us time to get to know one another. We didn't have the opportunity to talk last night."

She rendered a guilty smile, then released her right hand from the steering wheel, bringing it to rest on his knee. "I'm sorry about that. I really get into dancing—it's my exercise. Once I begin I can't stop."

"I see that."

"Anyway, it's always so crowded and so loud that if you try to talk, you can't have a conversation without yelling."

David topped her hand with his. "You have a good point there." He hesitated. "Please forgive me if I ask a question that is too personal or offends you."

She placed her right hand back on the wheel. "I don't anticipate that happening." She paused. "For some odd reason I feel very comfortable with you…and that scares me." She paused again. "I wouldn't have ever dreamed of inviting someone to the mountains for the weekend…much less someone I just met." She raised her right hand, pointing. "But I did tell you not to get your hopes up."

David brought up both hands, palms facing out, as if defending himself. "I'm a big boy…and I'm a Southern gentleman. If anything happens, it will be by your first move."

She smiled, dropping her hand back to his knee. "You are so sweet." She paused. "But first you tell me about yourself."

David wanted so much to tell her the entire truth, beginning with his true name. He felt so comfortable with her as well, strange as it was for them both. But his training was telling him no. So he didn't reveal his true name, but he told her a life story very similar to his own. "My mother died when I was just an infant. Her twin sister raised me as her own."

"I am so sorry," Sheridan said in a tender voice.

"Don't be," he responded. "I never knew it until just recently. I was loved dearly by my other mother, and I love her dearly as if she was my biological mother."

"Why did she wait until now to tell you?"

David turned towards the front windshield, gazing through the snow-spattered glass, sorrow filling his heart. "She passed away just before Thanksgiving. I read it in a letter she left me. She couldn't bear to tell me while she was alive, in fear that I may think of her differently."

Sheridan glanced at him then squeezed his knee gently, as if to let him know that she cared. "I didn't know." She hesitated, not knowing whether to ask or not. "Your father?"

"Dead," he lied, though it could be the truth, but he meant it for a lie. "It's okay…remember I'm a big boy." He focused his attention on her. "Now it's your turn…I want to hear about your spoiled life."

Sheridan's mouth dropped in shock, and then she clamped down on his knee with all her strength. "Take that back!"

"Okay, okay," he surrendered. "I mean tell me about the exciting life of a Senator's daughter."

They both laughed.

"I lived a normal life like everyone else."

"Hmmm," he commented. "Life in Manhattan, a second home on a mountain resort. Don't tell me…you probably have another house on the West Coast."

"Well…"

"Ah ha!"

"Not anymore…we had a home in Stanford where I went to college.

"You went to Stanford?" he asked in a shocked tone.

"Yes," she answered, saying it slowly. "I had a full scholarship here at Columbia, his alma mater. But I wanted to go away to school."

He gave her an I told you so look; she recognized it instantly. "I am not spoiled."

Then he said something quickly, without thought. "Daddy's little girl." He knew the instant it rolled off his tongue that it was a mistake. He wanted to quickly snatch it back out of the air, like a frog snatching a bug. By the expression on her face, it was way too late. She became stone-faced, glaring emotionless straight ahead. Silence filled the vehicle, the tension thick as butter. The sounds of the wipers, the back and forth swooshing, were the only sounds registering.

"I'm sorry," he finally muttered, not getting a response. "I guess the skiing lesson has been cancelled."

Her stone face cracked. "No…but the chances of you receiving a broken bone just rose considerably." She finally smiled. "No…you don't have anything to be sorry about."

David spoke to her in a very serious tone, like a cop. "You know that I am bound by law. Anything you say will be kept in the strictest confidence."

She looked over at his serious face then cracked up. "Okay…since you are bound by law." She hesitated. "I'm not close to my father, have not been for years now. That is why when he is at home for the weekend, I come up here. During the week my schedule is very busy. That plus my dancing keeps me well out of his sight. We hardly see one another, which is the way I want it. We are like two strangers living under the same roof."

David wanted to jump in and ask her about her mother, but he was reluctant after his last screw-up. Then as if she read his thoughts, she mentioned her mother. "It isn't much different from when I was growing up," she continued. "He left Mother and me alone most of the time. And there were always suspicions that he had numerous affairs. But he was never caught. When I was at Stanford, Mother would come out and live with me for months at a time. He never set foot out there. Mother bought the house and took care of everything. Then three years ago she just vanished. He had her laptop that she supposedly left behind. There was a Dear John letter on it to him. It said that she had met someone, and that she was moving out of the country, with a changed name, so he couldn't come after her." She paused. "I still don't believe it. She wouldn't have left me as well. I don't know what has happened to her." She hesitated. "After I graduated, I had planned to stay in Stanford and get a job as a lawyer. But he sold the house and got me a job in New York City. It was his way of forcing me into his life. I went along with it... partly because everything was in his name."

Silence returned. David turned to her. "Sounds like you need a good private detective."

Her smile returned, breaking the solemn look on her face. "Do you know where I can find a good one?"

"You're in luck. It just so happens that I do."

She glanced at him. "But can I afford him?"

"I think we can work out a trade."

Sheridan raised an eyebrow to him. He began to laugh, knowing what she must be thinking. "If you teach me how to ski...and not break my neck, then after I finish this case, I will take your case...pro bono."

"You got a deal...but I can't promise you about your neck."

They both laughed.

Chapter 14

Sheridan and David continued tracking north, falling deep into conversation, bonding, not realizing the time as it flew by. Just before lunch they reached Kingston, their turning point on the road, tracking then westward into the Catskill Mountains. They drove through the historic city, then down to the waterfront. Famished from all the conversation, they decided to grab a bite before tackling the mountains. Simultaneously, their eyes fell upon a red rustic building front with the appearance of a store from the 1950s, with a canopy in front stretching out to the sidewalk. The name on the front read Ship to Shore, an American Bistro.

After a memorable lunch, they hit the snowy road again. As they entered the mountains, David was mesmerized at the sheer beauty of the scenery, with white flakes from Heaven drifting downward to carpet majestic mountain tops. Sheridan took pleasure in witnessing his first reactions to snow-covered mountains, like a child going to the State Fair for the first time. As they finally approached their destination, Sheridan pointed up ahead to a driveway entrance cornered by a rock column ten feet high on each side. A large double gate of black iron filled the gap between the rock columns, with a large letter B in the center. "That driveway leads up to the house," she said as they whisked by.

David looked back at the entrance. "Where are we going?"

"To hit the slopes...of course."

"Did you have to use the word hit?" he asked in fright.

She smiled. "We have a few hours of daylight left."

"Okay," he stretched out the word. "That should be enough time to break a few bones."

Sheridan laughed.

The skiing went more smoothly than David had anticipated, and soon dusk began to fall over the mountain tops and valleys. Sheridan and David arrived at the house just as the automatic security lights flashed on. The house had a two-story gray timber frame with a full front porch. On one side connected to a dining area protruded a glass-covered sun room. To the rear, facing the glorious view of the snow-covered mountains, was a gigantic open patio. The interior was open to bedroom lofts overhead, encased by natural wood banisters overlooking the living room. A monstrous slate-rock fireplace was the center point of the house, with every room circling it. An oil painting of a distinguished-looking man hung in the center, her father Senator

Robert Blakely he assumed but would not dare ask. Gas log inserts sat within the fireplace, casting a romantic glow into the living room. Its shimmering flames reflected off the outer white semi-gloss walls. The house was flooded with handmade wooden furniture, leather chairs, sofa and recliners to match. In front of the fireplace, smothering practically the entire wooden floor in the living room, was a thick white fur rug. The air was filled with a mixture of leather and natural wood scents.

After they both showered, to the kitchen they headed. David prepared and cooked lamb chops, while Sheridan chopped up a fresh salad and popped a cork on a bottle of wine.

"That's what I forgot," David said, as the sound of the cork reminded him of something. "I should have brought us something to drink. I don't know how to make an apple martini, but I can make a delicious strawberry daiquiri."

Sheridan poured the wine. "There was no need... there is a wine cellar beneath us."

"Really," he responded, surprised as well as intrigued.

"It's the only original part of the house left. The house was entirely remodeled three years ago. But the temperature of the old basement is perfect and constant year round, perfect for a wine cellar. So that was left the way it was, and this new house was built over top of it. There are several hundred bottles stored down there. Some date back to the seventies."

After the meal and washing the dishes, they retired to the living room. Resting the glasses of wine on the fireplace hearth, they both stretched out on the plush white fur rug, each turning on their sides, facing each other. "Well," Sheridan said, looking David in his rich blue eyes. "Was I right?"

David's eyes narrowed, rendering a strange look. "Right about what?"

She smiled. "Snow skiing…don't you just love it?"

"I have to admit, I had a great time. But that was a real workout."

A devilish grin crept across her face. "So then…I guess you will be working for me after you solve this case."

David smiled. "A promise is a promise…and I have never backed down on a promise."

"Speaking of promises," she responded, as they then locked eyes. "I see you are not wearing a ring…you are not promised to someone?"

"It's complicated," he replied, breaking eye contact as he reached for his glass.

"Honesty…I like that in a man. You could have easily said no, but you are being truthful with me. I respect that." She took a short sip of wine. "How complicated?"

"I have a very close friend," he said as he set his glass back down. "We were high school sweethearts, then drifted apart during college. Now we both work in the same city. So we spend some time together, no commitments."

"So, you have a friend with benefits."

David blushed. "Is that the legal term for it nowadays?"

"If you are not committed...then you are a free agent," Sheridan responded. "Meaning...you are free for the taking."

Just then, David's phone vibrated. The two gazed into each other's eyes while the phone danced. Not wanting to, David checked the number. The look on his face told Sheridan that it was his friend with benefits, Kimberly. David glanced back to Sheridan. "Take it," she told him. "It's the right thing to do."

David answered. Sheridan quietly rose, then picked up the two wine glasses, downing hers as she carried them both to the kitchen. After washing them both, she slipped up the stairway. Unaware to David, she watched him for a few minutes from the banister overhead. After a few minutes, she faded away into a bedroom loft.

Forty-five minutes later, Sheridan walked out to the edge of the balcony, listening for conversation. The house was completely silent. She descended quietly to the living room, wearing only a thin blue gown. She stood over David as he lay sleeping, exhausted from snow skiing. She kneeled down by his side, kissing him gently on his cheek. Never stirring him, she quietly returned to her loft.

Chapter 15

David fell into a deep sleep, totally drained from the skiing adventure. He had never been one to dream, or at least to remember his dreams, but tonight was different. Exhaustion pulled him down into a deeper sleep than usual. Slowly his vision cleared, as he found himself in the house that he was now asleep in. Weirdly, as if an outer body experience, he watched himself sleeping on the thick white fur rug. He wore the same clothes he had on when talking to Sheridan. Then he recollected his last thought before drifting asleep, a phone conversation with Kimberly. Then the door to the wine cellar slowly creaked open. A breeze from the draft stirred everything inside the house, growing into a strong wind that shook the chandelier over the dining room table. Suddenly a beautiful woman appeared, standing over David while he still lay sleeping. She had long platinum blonde hair and was wearing a red low-cut dress. She stood silently over him, smiling down at him. The crimson-colored key, which he wore around his neck, then slipped out from under his shirt. Still connected to the silver chain, it drew towards her, as if drawn to a magnet. The crimson key suspended in midair at the end of the chain, drawn to its owner, Amber. David jumped to a sitting position.

"David!" Sheridan called from the banister above.

He looked up at her, still not sure if he was dreaming. She stood in a sexy light blue gown, in her otherwise obviously naked body. Silently he stared.

"David!" she repeated loudly. "Are you okay? I heard you jerking and talking in your sleep."

He rubbed his forehead. "Yes, I guess so...I was dreaming about my mother."

Not realizing which mother he was referring to, she mistakenly thought he meant Alice, who just passed. "It is understandable—you just lost her."

"I have never dreamed about her before."

"I dream of my mother often. But only when I'm here. You were extremely exhausted. You must have been in a deeper sleep than usual."

"Maybe so," he responded, rubbing his face and eyes.

"You don't have to sleep on the floor you know," she said, then hesitated long enough for thoughts to enter his mind of making love to her on the white fur rug.

Then she pointed across the room. "There is another bedroom over there."

He didn't even look in that direction, only gazed at her sleek sexy body, imagining her naked body beneath his. "Oh...thanks."

She turned, walking away, as he watched her body sway through the thin transparent gown. She quickly turned her head, catching him in the act, like once before. Then she gave him that same sexy smile as she did when she caught him before. Once she drifted out of sight, he returned to reality. He rose to his feet, taking off his shirt. The crimson key dangled on his chest. David reminisced about his dream as he walked slowly to the wine cellar door that opened mysteriously in his dream. Carefully he reached out for the doorknob, as if expecting it to suddenly blow wide open with his mother's ghost flying in with the wind. He drew his hand back, thinking to himself, "You dummy. There is no such thing as ghosts. It was just a dream, because I was tired." He then took the knob firmly with confidence, turning it and pulling the door open. It opened with ease, silently gliding on its hinges. "That's strange," he thought to himself. "It squeaked loudly in my dream. And the draft was very strong."

Thinking nothing else of it, except that it was just a dream, he flicked on the light. A dim light just above his head flickered on, illuminating just the stairs before him. He slowly descended down the short flight of wooden steps, each creaking at every step. Reaching the floor, he noticed a light bulb dangling from the ceiling with a pull chain attached. He pulled down gently on the old chain. Another dim light bulb jumped to life. With only his eyes, he surveyed the cellar. Straight ahead and continuing to his left was a wall filled with tools of all kinds, neatly hanging in their respective places, according to the shadow board behind them.

A six-foot-high wooden wine rack began at the right corner in front of him. It came straight out then made an L-shaped turn, heading another twenty feet into a cavern-shaped room. Wine racks filled the walls of this room, with hundreds of bottles resting undisturbed within their cradles. The air was 55 degrees according to a large thermometer mounted on a wooden support beam just in front of David's eyes.

After satisfying his curiosity, David pulled the old chain again, taking the life away from the light bulb he had just revived. As he took his first step upward, David had an overwhelming sense that someone was there in the darkness, watching him. He quickly turned, jerking the old chain to shed some light on his feelings. The light bulb danced to life, swaying back and forth, shedding minimal light into the dark shadows of the cavern-shaped room, but well enough for him to see that he was alone. He cast his eyes around the room, as the swaying light bulb finally came to rest. Nothing was visible to the naked eye, yet he still had a strong sense that someone or something was there, luring him to come closer. Even though he was strongly drawn, David dismissed his strange feelings, shutting off the light once again. Darkness quickly overtook the room, leaving nothing stranger than his thoughts.

David returned to the room above, slowly shutting the door behind him, and waited curiously for anything unexplainable. After a minute, he returned to the living room, standing in thought as he lifted the crimson key, gazing at it as if in a trance. A squeak broke his trance. His first thought was a ghost walking up the steps from the cellar. Then he returned to reality, "A ghost doesn't weigh enough to make a floor squeak. But how much does a ghost weigh? Wait a minute...there is no such thing as ghosts."

A second squeak sounded, only much closer this time. David spun around quickly, frozen in his tracks by what caused the squeak in the floor. Sheridan stood at arm's length in front of him, with only a thin blue translucent gown between them.

"Still dreaming?" she asked in a tender voice as she reached out, taking the crimson key in hand.

"Uh huh," he replied as his eyes fell down into her gown.

"This is beautiful," she said, inching closer.

"Very beautiful," he responded, to her not the key.

She then looked up into his eyes, dropping the gown to the floor.

"Are you making a move?" he asked, taking a deep swallow.

"No," she replied, looking deep into his eyes, leaning in to him, her warm breasts touching his bare chest. "Now I am."

They melted into each other.

Chapter 16

While David and Sheridan lay sleeping, after an intense round of exploring each other's bodies, Mike Scully lay sleeping peacefully at home in Brooklyn Heights. Peacefully maybe, but by no means quietly, for his snoring was enough to wake the dead. In this scenario, his snoring was loud enough for an intruder to break in without being heard. As Scully steadily sawed away, a masked man jimmied the door at the rear entrance. Once inside, he removed his disguise, strange as it may be, leaving it at the door with his snow-covered boots. He then maneuvered through the dark house as if he was familiar with the layout.

The half-moon from the clear sky above cast minimal light through the windows. Following the sound of a chain saw, he found his way into the bedroom where Scully lay sleeping unaware that he had company. Carefully, he leaned over Scully's body, taking hold of the pillow on the other side of the bed.

As he straightened up, with pillow in hand, Scully opened his eyes. Scully looked up at this intruder, with a look on his face as if he knew him, and wondered what he was doing. Without hesitation, the intruder quickly lowered the pillow, blanketing Scully's face. He forced his weight down against the pillow, making a perfect seal to prevent air from seeping out, and making it impossible for Scully's frail body to push him off. Scully struggled for a long agonizing minute, kicking and flopping like a fish out of water. Then his body gradually became still, as life surrendered to death.

Determined to ensure the inevitable, the assassin held a steady pressure on the pillow for another couple minutes. Releasing the pressure, he then checked for a pulse with a gloved hand. Sure of his victory, he peeled the pillow from Scully's pale wrinkled face, eyes and mouth wide open. Without remorse, the assassin closed Scully's mouth, then both eyes. He then walked back into the living room where a stand up ash tray sat. He picked up the ash tray, taking it into the bedroom, setting it conveniently close to where Scully's lifeless body lied. He then picked out a half-used cigar out of the ashes, placing it carefully between Scully's first and second fingers.

With a pocket penlight, the assassin slowly moved the light around the room, like a search light in a prison camp. The light stopped when it fell upon an old filing cabinet four drawers high. He walked to the filing cabinet with penlight in mouth and opened the top drawer. The old drawer scraped loudly as it opened. Fingering carefully through the files, he failed to locate what he came for. He forced the top drawer closed, then proceeded to the next. This drawer scraped louder than the first, binding to a halt about halfway open. He cursed under his breath as he tugged harder. Without success, he reached inside the jammed drawer, freeing it from what held it hostage, but not before a piece of pointed steel pierced the top of his hand.

The assassin shook his hand in pain while continuously cursing under his breath. Losing his temper, he kicked the hard cabinet, forgetting he was shoeless. Grimacing as well as cursing, he hobbled in a circle while waving his hand, like a one-legged duck with a broken wing trying to fly. Though still in pain from one end to the other, he managed to regain his composure. He picked up the penlight, which fell loose during the fiasco, then picked up where he left off.

The assassin searched diligently through the files until suddenly his movement ceased. Smiling around the penlight, he lifted a manila folder from the filing cabinet. He carefully set the folder down on the nightstand and began to inspect its contents. The thin beam of light from the pen revealed the name on the file, Amber Paige. While conducting a thorough scan of its contents, unknown to him, his wound steadily seeped blood through the tear in his glove. As he read, a single drop of blood dangled from the edge of his hand. He quickly closed the folder. The sudden movement freed the dangling drop of blood. It splattered silently on the wooden floor below.

With file in hand, the assassin hobbled his way to the bed. Reaching deep into his front pocket, he pulled out a butane lighter. Two flicks and the lighter came to life. He held the hot flame against the burnt end of the cigar, scorching the end and quilt as well. He hobbled back to the filing cabinet. He lit the file in his hand, watching it burn to halfway, then dropped it into the drawer on top of the other papers. The flame leaped instantly, as if an accelerant was used. He then hobbled quickly out the room, hesitating at the door, looking back one last time to make sure his victim would be burnt beyond recognition. Satisfied, he hobbled as quickly as he could to the rear door. Returning the mask to his face and boots to his feet, he hobbled his way into the darkness.

Chapter 17

David and Sheridan woke the next morning, taking up where they left off during the wee hours of morn. By noon they had managed to escape from under the covers. They both prepared a late breakfast of bacon and eggs. "What's on the agenda for today?" David asked, though really preferring just rest.

Sheridan dug deep into her jean pocket, retrieving two small sets of keys. Smiling, she held them in the air, jingling them. "I bet you have never driven a snow mobile before."

His eyes widened. "I don't believe I have... They don't do too well on the sandy beaches back home."

About that time, his phone jumped to life. He checked the caller id.

"Is that your F-W-B?" Sheridan asked.

David grinned. "No," stretching the word out. "It's my J-O-B."

David recognized the number, Moreno. "Hello Moreno…I thought you were off this weekend."

"I was," Moreno solemnly responded. "Got some bad news. Mike Scully is dead."

David quickly sat up in the chair. "What happened?"

Moreno hesitated. "House fire, his body was found in bed…at least we assume it's his body. The medical examiner is confirming it as we speak. The body was burnt beyond recognition."

"I'm sorry to hear that," David said. "He seemed like a good man. I could tell the two of you were close."

"He was a damn fine detective too." Moreno paused. "I don't like the way this feels."

"It's hard to lose someone close."

"Yes," Moreno interrupted. "But that is not what I was referring to… It looks fishy if you know what I mean."

"How so?"

"Fifteen years ago Scully lost his brother. He fell asleep in bed while smoking. Ever since then, Scully has never, I mean never, smoked in his bedroom, much less while in bed." He paused. "The ash tray was setting by the bed. Scully only smoked in his recliner…and that was only when watching a game. The ash tray has never been moved except to clean. Hell, there were permanent imprints from the stand on that fancy rug he has in the living room. I don't like it…I just don't like it at all."

"Is there going to be an investigation?" David asked, while helping Sheridan with the dishes.

"Not sure yet," Moreno answered. "We are waiting for the fire marshal to determine the cause. The family believes he was smoking while in bed, not me. They aren't even asking for an autopsy." Moreno paused. "Where are you anyway? I went by your hotel. They said you had checked out just for the weekend."

David hesitated. "I'm snow skiing in the Catskill Mountains."

"Oh yeah," Moreno remarked. "With who?"

David grinned, casting an eye towards Sheridan. "It's politics."

Sheridan gave him an eye, then smiled and shook her head. Moreno laughed, realizing what the code word meant. "No way…the Senator's daughter. Man you are moving up in the world."

David grinned, trying to hold back his laughter. Then he discarded the smile, acting in a serious manner. "Yes…I should finish my work today and will be driving back late tonight. You can brief me first thing in the morning." David could hear Moreno's laughter as he ended the call. Suddenly a small set of keys hit David in the chest and dropped to the floor. He glanced at the keys on the floor, and then looked up at Sheridan.

"Politics," she said. "Is that the legal term for it nowadays?"

They both smiled. They bundled up and headed outdoors. The sky was a clear baby blue with barely a cloud in the sky, but still cold, a balmy twenty degrees. The fluffy white powder was about two feet deep, nearly up to their knees. About a hundred feet from the house, bordered by thick pines weighted down heavily by snow, sat an outdoor building the size of a two-car garage. The color of the siding matched the gray timber framed house. To the front was a large garage door and a small entrance door at the corner.

Sheridan unlocked the side door and disappeared inside. A few seconds later, the electric garage door rose slowly, unveiling two metallic purple Polaris 600 snowmobiles. "What do you think?" Sheridan asked, holding an outstretched hand towards the sleek machines.

"They are beauties," he replied. "You still promise not to break my neck?"

"I don't make promises I cannot keep," she responded, while cranking one snowmobile. "Hop on...I will take you for a spin so you can see how it's done. Then I will bring you back for the other one. Then the games will begin."

David slowly approached the humming machine and carefully threw a leg over. He sat up close behind Sheridan, wrapping his arms around her thin waist, reminiscing about last night. He watched her lips move as she instructed him on how to operate the snowmobile. Without warning, she blasted into the white wonderland, almost throwing him off the back. She held nothing back as they blistered through the snow at what appeared to him about 100 mph. They circled the small valley lined with tall pine trees, snow clinging to the branches, pushing them closer to the snow-covered ground. The wind blew in spurts, and snow from the tree limbs fell with the appearance of a snowstorm. Sheridan came to an abrupt stop. "Okay switch up."

They traded places, and she held him tight around his waist. "I like this," David said, glaring over his shoulder at her.

"There is no time for politics," she remarked with a grin. "See if you can handle this baby."

David hit the throttle and the machine jumped. He twisted and turned, like a child learning to ride a bike without the training wheels for the first time. By the time they made it back to the house, he was handling it like a pro. Sheridan hopped off and fired the other one up. She pulled up alongside of him. "Now follow me… if you think you can."

Sheridan shot out in front of David, blowing snow into his face. She glanced over her shoulder at him while laughing. He gunned the snow machine and the chase was on. They played in the snow all afternoon until dusk approached. Then they left the cold behind, entering the warm cozy house and warming their hands and bodies in front of the fireplace. They both retreated upstairs and into the shower, together. Continuing their shared passion, they made love before the journey back to reality, New York City.

Chapter 18

Monday morning came bitterly cold with a bone-chilling breeze. David stepped into police headquarters, doughnuts in hand. Moreno was not at his desk, nor the rest of the detectives. Just as David poured himself a cup of steaming hot coffee, detectives and uniformed cops filed in from a room at the rear. David poured another cup then headed to Moreno's desk, where Moreno had fallen behind his computer screen. "What's up?" David asked, handing a cup to Moreno.

"Just got out of a meeting," Moreno replied. "The fire marshal ruled that the fire started in two places. A small blaze began on the bed. Another much larger blaze began in the filing cabinet. And yesterday the medical examiner couldn't find any evidence that Scully died from smoke inhalation. His lungs were free of smoke. They are performing a full autopsy as we speak. They are ruling the death as suspicious. A CSI team is on the scene right now."

David blew on his hot coffee, then took a cautious sip. "I hope I wasn't the cause of this."

Moreno raised an eye. "What do you mean?"

"Well, we did talk to Scully on Friday about my case," David said, pulling a doughnut out of the bag. "He gave us some valuable information out of his filing cabinet...information that has conveniently disappeared from the Dungeon. And now he is dead... and the information burned to a crisp. And my boss called this morning to tell me that someone from New York City has been checking my credentials."

"That seems too coincidental," Moreno remarked. Then his face hardened as Pete Sullivan stepped up.

"Moreno," Sullivan said. "Scully and I go way back. If there is anything I can do to help with the investigation, just let me know."

Moreno stared Sullivan in the face just as the phone rang. With eyes still locked on Sullivan, Moreno picked up. "Hello," Moreno said, then listened. "That's great. Get it to the lab right away... Great job, thanks again." Moreno hung up. "Great news—they have found a drop of blood on the floor. It's in the lab now. We should have the results soon."

Sullivan's expression turned pale as he stepped away in silence. David and Moreno watched him go. "Why is he limping?" David asked, biting into a doughnut.

"I could care less," Moreno replied, taking a chunk out of his doughnut. "Broken toe I heard."

In a penthouse suite, downtown Manhattan, a well-dressed man sat at a table, sipping on coffee and reading the morning paper. The headline before his eyes read,

Death of Retired Detective Deemed Suspicious. The man pulled out his Blackberry, whipping his thumb across the face, speed dialing a preloaded number. A phone vibrated in Pete Sullivan's pocket—not his regular cell, the one attached to his belt, but rather an untraceable one tucked in his shirt pocket. "Hello," Sullivan answered.

"You are getting sloppy in your old age," the well-dressed man said in an angered voice.

"Nothing to worry about—everything is under control," Sullivan assured him in a shaky voice.

"Under control!" the man snapped. "There wasn't any smoke in his lungs, you idiot! Why didn't you blow smoke down his throat?"

"Listen," Sullivan responded, trying to calm him down. "There is no need to worry. Moreno is working the case. I just talked to him. We will be working the case together. So if anything comes up I can take care of it."

"Nothing else had better come up."

Sullivan hesitated, sweat balls forming on his forehead. "There is one small obstacle I have to take care of."

A silent moment passed. "How small is this obstacle?"

Sullivan hesitated again, wiping his drenched forehead. "They found a drop of blood at the scene... it is mine."

"What the hell!" the man yelled, banging his clinched fist on the table, sloshing coffee out of his cup.

"I doubt if they can tie it back to me," Sullivan said, nervously. "There was too much heat and smoke damage. I have a good alibi if I need one…I was helping with the Amber Paige case. And I checked out this David Peoples. He is a private detective. He and Moreno asked me about the Amber Paige case…so that is why I went to see Scully."

The phone went silent for a moment. All Sullivan heard was the man's angry breathing. "Have you found out who hired this David Peoples?"

Sullivan hesitated. "I'm working on that… He was out of town for the weekend."

The phone went silent again for a few moments. "I will get someone to work on this David Peoples… You need to lay low for a while. Concentrate on this case and be as helpful as much as you can. I'm still waiting for my email on this David Peoples."

Relieved, Sullivan replied, "That might be a good idea. I will keep you informed. And I will get that email to you within the hour."

"You do that," the man demanded, then ended the call. He rose and walked over to a large window with a picturesque view of the Manhattan skyline. The bright orange morning sun blazed fiery reflections off the snow-covered building tops and steeples. Gazing out through the frosted window, he pulled out a small faded black leather address book that was cracked and worn. After spotting the number he desired, he made a call. On the third ring, a deep raspy voice answered. The well-dressed man said, "I have a job for you."

Back at police headquarters, Moreno and David had come to the conclusion that both cases were linked, so they investigated both as one. They found that the Glamorous Modeling Agency was no longer in business, having shut its doors years ago when the economy took a turn for the worse. They did manage to find that it began in 1985, with eight fresh young faces to the industry. One of the fresh young faces was that of Miss Amber Paige, an up and rising star according to an article in the Times. The day wound down quickly, but it had led to numerous possibilities.

Moreno suddenly blackened the computer screen, spotting Sullivan making a wounded approach. "Moreno," Sullivan said. Moreno closed his notes. "Any leads on the Paige case?"

Moreno instantly shook his head. Then, as if a real pro, he lied. "No luck at all—just dead ends everywhere we turn."

David was well aware of the game Moreno was playing, a game usually played against a suspect or someone under interrogation, not with a fellow detective, unless he was despised.

"I came over here to tell you something," Sullivan said, having a difficult time maintaining eye contact as Moreno obviously was uninterested in what he had to say. "After you asked me about the Amber Paige case on Friday, I went to see Scully the next morning, Saturday."

Moreno raised an eye to Sullivan, suddenly interested, giving his undivided attention. Sullivan met his stare. "I went by to ask him if he remembered anything about the Amber Paige case from 1986."

Moreno's eyes narrowed. "So…" He paused, glaring intently. "Are you saying that you were the last person to see Scully alive?"

Sullivan returned Moreno's glare, anger filling his voice. "I'm not going to fall into that trap. How dare you use that on me. What am I...a suspect now?"

Moreno stood his ground and grinned. "Depends on how you answer my question."

"Hell no!" Sullivan snapped back. "He was fine when I left him. You know damn well that the killer was the last one to see Scully alive."

Moreno's grin evolved into a smile. "You know as well as I do...that everyone is a suspect at first."

Sullivan jabbed a finger at him, like pointing a loaded gun. "Look, I don't need this bull...I came over here to try and help. And you treat me as a suspect."

Angry, Sullivan hobbled towards the door, Moreno watching every crooked step. "Hey Sullivan!"

Sullivan stopped just before reaching the door. He turned and stared at Moreno, red-faced from anger. "What!"

"You never said what Scully told you when you asked him about the case."

"Nothing!" Sullivan spit out. "It was a long time ago...he couldn't remember anything about the case."

Moreno cast an eye to David. "I guess you are right, it was too long ago...Thanks Buddy."

Sullivan gave Moreno the finger, then disappeared through the door.

"That was real strange," David remarked. "He just drowned himself in lies. I now see why you were playing that game with him."

"Sneaky little bastard," Moreno remarked. "He hated Scully...and the feelings were mutual. That is why I can't trust him. Scully warned me about him years ago." He paused. "With his lies, he is the best suspect we have." The phone rang. Moreno answered, "Hello, yes…what you got?"

David watched Moreno's facial expression quickly turn to surprise, then amazement just before he hung up. "Bingo! We got our first major suspect."

"Oh yeah…who?"

Moreno smiled wide. "Mr. Pete Sullivan—that was his blood at the crime scene. C'mon, let's catch him in the parking lot. He has some explaining to do."

Moreno took off like a horse out of the gate at the Kentucky Derby. In a very fast-paced walk, he led David out of the building. Moreno pointed at Sullivan getting into his navy blue Chevy Malibu, parked at the rear of the parking lot. David followed close behind the doughnut king, never dreaming it possible he could move so quickly. Moreno's jacket tail waved behind him as he hurried along, like the tail on a race horse. Sullivan, not aware that he was being pursued, fumbled with his car keys.

Sullivan managed to slip the key into the ignition. Then he raised his eyes and met Moreno's determined stare with David close behind, within a stone's throw. David was suddenly struck by Moreno's body, blown backwards by an explosion, driving them both to the ground. An explosion the force of ten sticks of dynamite ripped through the once blue Malibu, sending a fireball at least three stories high, accompanied by body parts—the auto's and Sullivan's. Metal splinters and shards of glass pierced through the air like tiny missiles of destruction, blistering everything in their path, including Moreno. The explosion shattered glass in nearby cars in the parking lot, rattling the windows of headquarters as well.

David sat up bewildered, taking notice that his jacket, shirt and tie were spattered with blood. A quick self-examination revealed that he was not injured. He turned to Moreno, whose body lay motionless on its side. David carefully rolled Moreno over and saw his face riddled with broken glass, blood running from his nose and ears. Horrified, David checked for a pulse. Moreno's heart was beating, but weakly, and he was unresponsive. David spotted uniforms racing to the scene. "Help! We need an ambulance!"

Chapter 19

Five hours later, Moreno woke slowly in the ICU of the New York Downtown Hospital, his life as well as his vision blurred. His first clear picture was the pretty round face of his wife, Angie, a short thick lady with dark brown hair and eyes to match. He found himself the recipient of a major concussion, with numerous lacerations, none life-threatening. He was a very lucky man—a few feet closer and he would now be lying in the morgue instead of a hospital bed. His recollection of the incident was just a blur, partly due to the concussion and partly due to heavy medications. David had been in the waiting room since Moreno was admitted, still wearing the blood-spattered shirt, having discarded his tie and jacket. A nurse exited Moreno's room. "How is he?" David asked.

"He just came to," she answered, never breaking her stride.

Without permission, David snuck in. The nurse had said that he came to, but he was lying still with his eyes shut, Angie clutching his hand. David walked up quietly to her. "How is he?" he whispered.

"Starving to death," Moreno replied with his eyes shut. "Did you bring doughnuts?"

Angie patted his hand. "You silly fool."

"I'm glad he's coming around," David said to Angie.

"Yes, but he is very weak," she responded, never taking her eyes off him.

"I can see that…I will come back to check on him in the morning," David said, then quietly turned.

"Will you be alone?" Moreno asked in a weak raspy voice.

David smiled, knowing what he really meant. "No…I will have a couple with me when I come." David watched a familiar smile growing on Moreno's bandaged face. "You get some rest now."

"He will," Angie remarked. "I will make sure of that."

Just as David left the room, his phone vibrated. Glancing at the caller ID, he recognized the number. "Well hello darling."

"David!" Sheridan blurted out in panic. "Are you all right? I have been working. I heard about the explosion earlier, but I just heard that Moreno was taken to the hospital."

"I'm fine," he replied, taking a seat in the waiting room. "I was knocked a little silly for a moment."

"And Moreno?"

"He just woke up for the first time. He has a bad concussion and cuts on his face from flying debris."

"That's a good sign, him waking up," she responded. "What happened?"

David cast an eye around the room. "I believe we are uncovering something big. Scully and Sullivan were the two detectives working on a missing person report twenty-five years ago. The same one I am looking into. Now they have both been murdered and the files are missing. Someone is going to a lot of trouble to keep something a secret."

"Could this be tied to the Mafia?"

"I am not ruling out anything at this point. If it is not them, then it is someone with a lot of power."

Sheridan hesitated. "Are you in danger?"

"I'm not sure, but if I'm not…then I soon will be."

"What is that supposed to mean?"

David surveyed the room again. "Moreno and I made some progress today. And we were about to nail Sullivan when someone beat us to the blow. Sorry, I shouldn't have said it that way. I also have a list of people to question. If I stumble across some valuable information…then someone else might get hurt. And that someone could be me."

"I don't like the sound of that," Sheridan remarked. "I kinda like having you around. And I'm looking forward to you working my case…pro bono."

David laughed. "Is that what they call it nowadays? I kinda like being around too. I'm looking forward to working really close with you."

Sheridan sighed. "When can I see you?"

"Soon," David answered. "But I don't want you in harm's way. So it will be best if we try to keep it a secret…for your safety." He paused. "Are you free Wednesday evening?"

"Why yes," she replied excitedly. "I don't have anything after 3 p.m."

"I will think of something," David said. "I will call you when I have."

"Okay darling…can't wait."

The next morning David made a pit stop at a small coffee shop on his way to the hospital. A few minutes later, he escaped with two doughnuts hidden in a plain white paper bag, easily hidden underneath his jacket. When David entered Moreno's room, his wife Angie was faithfully still by his side. Moreno was sitting up in bed, more coherent than the evening before, but his face was swollen, accompanied by two black eyes from the sudden force.

"Honey…I would like you to meet someone," Moreno said to Angie. "This is David…" He paused, catching himself before revealing David's real name. "Peoples. He is a private detective from Charleston, South Carolina. And he is a friend."

David shook her tiny hand, each smiling to the other, while he kept the doughnuts cleverly hidden. "Angie, it is a pleasure."

"The pleasure is all mine," she responded.

David glanced at Moreno. "How is he doing?"

"Better…complaining about everything."

Moreno spotted the hidden treasure. "Hey Honey, David can keep me company for a while. Why don't you go to the cafeteria and have some breakfast."

Angie stared at him. "What are you up to? Sounds like you are trying to get rid of me."

"No Honey," Moreno said. "It's not like that, but I do need to discuss something with David."

She pointed a finger at him. "You are not supposed to be working…doctor's orders."

Moreno looked at David. "She is my Guardian Angel." He turned his attention towards her. "Talking is not working, now is it? Believe me, I definitely don't feel good enough to jump out of bed and hit the streets of New York City."

Angie made eye contact with David. He nodded his head to Angie. "Okay," she said slowly. "But if he tries to get out of bed, you shoot him."

Moreno tried to hold back his laughter because it was too painful. She kissed him on the only bare spot on his forehead that didn't have a bandage covering it. "Love you."

"Love you too, Honey," Moreno replied, watching her fade away through the doorway. Once she was out of sight, he looked at David. "All right, hand it over."

David handed him the bag with two doughnuts inside. Moreno took a peek inside and smiled through his pain. He slowly opened his mouth, just enough to squeeze a portion of the doughnut through. He closed his eyes as the splendid flavor mingled with his taste buds. "Do you know why they make doughnuts circular shaped with a hole in the middle?"

David laughed. "That is one question I can honestly say I have not dwelled on. Why?"

"Because it is heavenly food."

David gave him a confused stare. Moreno smiled, and then held a doughnut over his head. "It's made to resemble a halo."

David smiled while Moreno held a straight face, not because it was too painful to smile, but because he believed it to be true. "What do you remember about yesterday?" David asked.

Moreno grimaced as he swallowed. "It was all a blur until this morning. Now I picture it as if it is happening…Sullivan's face, and the sudden guilty look that fell over it when he saw us approaching. It was like he knew he was caught. Then a ball of fire and a feeling like I had been hit by a truck head on. Nothing else until I woke up with Angie by my side." Moreno gave David a confused stare of his own. "How did you get by without a scratch? You were right there with me."

"Yes, but I was behind you…trying to keep up with you."

"Oh," Moreno responded. "So I was your human shield."

David grinned and nodded. "But I did break your fall."

"Gee…thanks Buddy." They both laughed out loud, somewhat. David gave Moreno a serious look. "Who do you think could be responsible for this?"

Moreno stared in thought. "Scully always told me not to trust Sullivan. He had been seen talking to some shady characters, and some in limousines. There is no telling what connections he had made over the years."

"But to kill a cop…a man you used to work with who had your back in trouble. How can someone do that?"

"Money," Moreno replied. "And probably a ton of it…so he probably wasn't dealing with lowlifes. Whoever this is has plenty of money. But what puzzles me is what are they trying to hide that is worth killing for? And what does this have to do with your mother?"

"That is what I plan to find out," David replied.

Moreno dug into the bag. "Let me eat this one before my little angel returns." He took a bite. "What is your game plan?"

David reached behind his neck. "We came up with a list of people I need to question. But first I want to find out what this key fits." He pulled the chain out from under his shirt, revealing a crimson-colored key. Moreno carefully took the key. "Why is this key so important?"

"According to my mother, it holds the answer to her demise."

Moreno swallowed the last sweet morsel. "Then I suggest you find out what this key fits. There is a locksmith on the corner of Tompkins Square Park, 155 Avenue." He held the chain up in the air, rolling it back and forth between his fingers. The crimson key twirled one way then the other. The light from overhead shed a reflection on the glossy red crimson paint, causing it to sparkle as it spun. "You know what a wise old man once told me," Moreno said, gazing at the spinning key, as if hypnotized. "Life is filled with mysteries, some which are never solved. But all mysteries can be solved, even the most unusual ones, but only if you possess the correct key."

Chapter 20

In a Manhattan penthouse suite, the same well-dressed man sat at his table drinking coffee and reading the morning paper. The headline glaring in front of him read, Explosion Rocks Police Headquarters, Detective Dead. He set the paper down, took a sip of his steaming hot coffee, and then casually pulled out his Blackberry. He whipped his thumb across the screen and waited momentarily. A long list of emails popped up before his eyes. He chose the one he was searching for. He smiled widely as a picture of David Peoples filled his screen. He then made a call, which was answered on the third ring. A deep raspy voice answered, "Hello."

"I have a job for you, double the pay... His name is David Peoples."

David left Moreno in the safe custody of his wife, Angie. He stepped out of the hospital to hail a cab. He took notice of the Christmas decorations, reminiscing of Christmas when he was a boy. Alice, the only mother he knew, always made it the best time of the year. Though he had outgrown the thrill he knew as a child, he was saddened that this Christmas would be much different without his mother.

David was awakened from his trance by something striking his shoes. Looking down, he discovered they had been splattered with brown slushy snow from the cab he just hailed. David stomped off the slush and climbed into the cab, giving the driver his destination, Tompkins Square Park, 155 Avenue. The driver was dark-skinned with dark hair to match, a foreigner who spoke fluent English. David took in a little sightseeing through the crusty window. They passed right by the famed Madison Square Gardens. David got a thought—maybe after he found out what happened to his mother he would get Sheridan to introduce him to this great city. He wanted to visit the Statue of Liberty, ride to the top of the Empire State Building, and visit Ground Zero, just to mention a few.

Meanwhile, back at David's room, a lone man in a heavy brown overcoat opened the door. He had his collar turned up and a hat pulled down covering his face. The man checked up and down the empty hallway then slowly entered. Once inside, he moved quickly around the room, opening every door and every drawer with gloved hands. He rummaged through each, closely inspecting all of David's personal possessions. A sound from the hallway spooked him. He slowly pulled out a black handgun with a silencer attached. He slinked to the door like a cat, and then cracked it to take a peek. A cleaning cart set in the open doorway of the first room down the hall. He eased the door shut then proceeded to search the room. Suddenly he stopped, hearing the cleaning person at the room directly across the hall. The man concluded his business with the intent to leave the room the way it was, undisturbed, as if no one had been here. He eased to the door, cracking it ever so slightly. With silencer in hand, he watched the cleaning lady in the adjacent room. She disappeared into the bathroom. He quickly hid the gun and slipped out undetected, walking swiftly towards the stairs.

"Excuse me!" a female voice with a Hispanic accent yelled.

The man screeched to a halt, and then he turned slowly, seeing a round-faced dark-haired lady in a cleaning outfit.

"Would you like your room cleaned?"

The man quickly slipped on a fake smile. "Why yes, thank you… I would appreciate it."

"I clean your room after me clean this," she said, then slipped back into the room.

The man approached the room, surveying his surroundings while slipping his hand inside his overcoat. He slipped into the bathroom behind her, undetected. She rose up from cleaning the sink, spotting the gun and his face from their reflections in the mirror. Horror filled her eyes. The man held a finger to his lips, signaling for her to stay quiet. She felt the cold steel from the barrel of the gun resting on the back of her head. Tears flowed swiftly down her round cheeks just as he squeezed the trigger. A sudden swoosh then a dull thud sounded, followed by blood and brains filling the mirror and wall. The short round body drifted to the floor, blood rushing from the wound. The man moved quickly to the open door, wiping the blood from the barrel of his gun with a clean white towel. The blood-stained towel floated to the floor just as the man disappeared through the door to the stairway.

The cab with David inside pulled over to the curb with the driver pointing ahead to the locksmith shop. David paid his fare then trod the crowded street to the shop. A young narrow-faced man approached him. "May I help you?"

David pulled out the crimson key. "Yes, I wish to find out what this key fits into."

The young man stared at the key through round thick spectacles. "I think this is a job for Mick." Then he pointed to a hallway. "Second office on your right."

David thanked him and headed towards the hallway. He found the door and peered inside. A grey-haired man with glasses sat studying a computer screen. David rapped on the side of the doorway. "Excuse me...I was told that you may be able to help me."

The man stood to greet David with a hand. "My name is Domhnall McDougal."

"David Peoples," David replied while they shook hands. "Your name again?"

McDougal laughed. "That's all right, just call me Mick. My mother, God rest her soul, was Irish. She blessed me with her grandfather's name...or should I say cursed me."

David smiled while pulling out the crimson key. He held the chain up with the key dangling. Mick stared at it. "Ahh... 'Tis a fine-looking key you got there."

"I was wondering if you could tell me what it goes to."

"Off the top of my head, I would say an antique trunk." He sat and turned to the computer. "Oh fooey...I hate computers. Give me a book any day. Where the hell did they come up with the word google...sounds like baby talk if you ask me." He rose and took a large book from a shelf, then opened it revealing hundreds of pictures of antique keys. "Let's see if I can be more specific for you." He thumbed through numerous pages until he stopped on a page with pictures of keys similar to the crimson key. "Here we go," he said, holding the crimson key close to the page for comparison. "This is what you got...I was right, it's a key to an antique trunk. According to this, it's an Excelsior trunk, a Saratoga or Bride trunk, which is generally larger than normal. It dates back between the 1920s to 1940s. Some of these trunks have rounded tops where others have flat tops. The flat tops make great coffee tables. Most of them, the nicer models, have many compartments and trays. Some actually have secret compartments for storing valuables."

David stared at the pictures of the keys. "I don't see any red keys."

McDougal held the key up to where he could focus through the bifocal part of his glasses. He carefully studied the crimson key, turning it to every side. "For some reason this key has been painted. It appears to be with fingernail polish." He pointed his finger along the edges. "See here, the edges are silver, its original color. The fingernail polish has worn off the edges…I don't understand why someone would paint the key. Where did you get it?"

David fastened the key back around his neck. "It belongs to a missing person from twenty-five years ago…and somehow this key will unlock this mystery."

Chapter 21

David checked his notes on the key as he walked out of the door from the locksmith shop. His cell jumped in his pocket. "Hello," David said while hailing a cab.

"Where are you David?" Moreno asked.

"I just found out what this key fits…"

Moreno cut him off. "Spare me the details for later. You need to high foot it back to your hotel. I just got word that there has been a murder there."

David crammed the cell into his pocket while stepping out into the street, forcing a cab to stop. Flashing his credentials, he instructed the driver to double time it to the Hilton New York. By the time he reached the hotel, it was swarming with cops. David slipped through the dense crowd, making his way to the elevator, then up to the floor where his room was located. Exiting the elevator, he made eye contact with Moreno's boss, Lieutenant Jacoby, who stood in the doorway of the crime scene directly across the hall from

David's room. Jacoby waved David over. "I understand that you stay here," Jacoby said, pointing across the hall to a closed door.

David peeked in the door at the crime scene. "Yes sir I do."

Jacoby shook his head. "Ever since you got into town, there have been dead bodies piling up around you."

David strained to get a closer look inside. "I wish it weren't true. What have you got here?"

"Cleaning lady shot point blank in the back of her head. He or she must have snuck up behind her. No possible motive unless she saw something she wasn't supposed to."

David inched his way inside, witnessing the blood-drenched mirror and wall. The body had been taken away, but a chalk outline of the body remained. Jacoby walked up to David. "How long have you been gone from your room?"

Checking his watch, David replied, "About six hours. I left around eight. I went by the hospital, took Moreno some doughnuts." Jacoby shook his head. "Left straight from there," David continued. "I have been checking on a lead. Do you think this is somehow tied to my case?"

"So far we haven't come up with any motives," Jacoby replied. "Maybe he was looking for you, and she got a good look at him. How about taking a look in your room to see if anything is missing?"

David's hand dove into his pocket, retrieving his room key. He and Jacoby entered his room. At first glance it appeared as he had left it. Then David noticed a drawer that wasn't completely shut. He could not have left it that way—his mother drilled him about leaving drawers open when he was a child. David walked up to the dresser and stared down at the drawer. "Someone has been here."

"Don't touch a thing," Jacoby suddenly said. "I want this room dusted and worked as well."

David decided to head to the hospital to check on Moreno and fill him in on the events of the day. He hailed a cab and was off. Upon arrival, he walked through the automatic entrance doors with a direct shot to the elevator near the lobby desk. Just as he entered the elevator, a man in a heavy brown overcoat entered through the automatic doors. He slowly approached the information desk, carefully surveying his surroundings as he walked. A volunteer, a short thin senior lady with a tall silver beehive hairdo, sat behind the desk wearing a big smile. The man asked for Ricardo Moreno's room, which she freely gave. He thanked her and asked for directions to the stairway. She pointed a crooked finger and he headed that way.

Moreno's wife, Angie, sat loyally by Moreno's bed, facing the door. She landed an eye on David the second he stepped in. Before he could speak, David found her finger pointing at him. "Did you bring in doughnuts this morning?"

Stunned, David stared helplessly at Moreno.

"She saw the evidence around my mouth," Moreno said in a guilty tone.

David glanced back at Angie. Her eyes narrowed, not cracking a grin. "Guilty as charged," he admitted. "But I was forced against my will."

She jerked her stare around, landing it full force on Moreno. All he could do was hold a smile at her while he said to David, "Thanks for having my back…Buddy."

The three laughed out loud.

"Okay you two," Moreno painfully said. "Stop laughing…it hurts too much." He looked at David. "Details…I want all the dirty details."

David took a seat. "The murder at the hotel was a cleaning maid. She was cleaning the room across from mine. Someone popped her from behind while she was cleaning the bathroom, point blank in the back of the head."

A strange look blanketed Moreno's face. "Do you think the two cases are connected?"

David slowly nodded. "I do now…someone had been in my room. Nothing was taken, but someone was definitely snooping around. She must have seen him, so he took care of a loose end."

Moreno sat higher in bed, drowning in deep thought. "I have a theory… A private detective by the name of David Peoples is looking into a twenty-five-year old missing person case. Someone who knows what happened to this person is gradually and permanently removing all the pieces to the puzzle. This person has to be wondering after all this time who would hire a private eye to look into this."

"You are probably right," David agreed. "That is why someone went through my room, trying to find out who hired me."

Moreno met David's eyes. "You had better watch your back. This person may come after you. He can't afford to whack you off...at least not until he knows who hired you. He could make an attempt to beat it out of you."

The man wearing the heavy brown overcoat walked by Moreno's room, stopping in the nearby waiting area. He came to rest in a corner seat, perched with a bird's eye view of the hallway and Moreno's door. He opened a newspaper, cleverly using it to disguise his face, as he constantly peered just over the edge of the paper, down the hall and to Moreno's door.

David rose quietly, then walked towards the door. "Where are you going?" Moreno asked.

"To cover my ass...I'll be right back," David replied, slipping into the hall. He looked up and down in both directions, not realizing that he was being watched. David turned towards the man, who slipped his eye back behind a corner of the paper. David walked into the waiting area and approached the drink machine. He dug into his pocket then dropped in the change. He pushed a button and a can drink toppled down into the tray. David took it out and popped the top, proceeding to take a drink while viewing the occupants of the room.

An older couple sat together holding hands and whispering. A young red-headed girl just learning to walk bobbled around David's feet. The parents sat nearby with two boys, one with hair matching the girl's. Then David's eye landed on the man in the corner, a newspaper masking his face. David noticed that the paper had been in the same position since he first saw him after leaving Moreno's room. David studied him for a moment or two while draining the drink can. He caught a mere corner of the man's eye every so often, before it faded behind the paper once again. David crumpled the empty can in his hand, then dispensed of it into a nearby recycling container. He returned to Moreno's room.

"How's your ass?" Moreno asked.

Humored, David said, "There is one suspicious character in the waiting area."

"Oh yeah…how suspicious?"

David cracked the door and peeked. "A man I think was watching me from behind a newspaper." He didn't see the man anymore. "Maybe not…he's gone now."

Chapter 22

The man wearing the heavy brown overcoat hailed a cab. The cab stopped at the curb just in front of the entrance. The man crawled in the back. "Where you go?" a Hispanic driver asked.

"Nowhere," the man replied.

Confused, the driver turned to look at the man. The man in the back held up five crisp new one hundred dollar bills. The driver glared at the cash, like a hungry wolf staring down a rabbit.

"I want you to wait right here," the man said. He gave the driver David's description to a tee. He told him of an alley between there and David's hotel. He showed the driver another hand filled with five more crisp one hundred dollar bills, telling him that he would give him the other when he picked him up in the middle of the alley.

"Si Senoir," the driver said, then took the five out of the first hand, folding them in half and securing them in his front shirt pocket.

Thirty minutes later, David walked out of the hospital. It was dark now, much colder than earlier. A sharp breeze sliced through his thin jacket and tie. "You need ride!" a man yelled.

David looked in the direction of the voice. A Hispanic man stood just outside the driver side door of his cab, holding up a hand. David waved back and rushed in his direction. He jumped into the back seat, escaping the bitter cold. He then gave the driver the name of his hotel. David pulled out his notebook that was hidden inside a secret pocket of his jacket. He took his handy penlight and clicked it on. Holding it between his teeth, he turned to a page with six names written on it. These were the six models Amber worked with, presumed to be alive. David planned to start investigating them the next day.

David felt the cab turning too soon to be at the hotel. He raised his head just as he placed the book back out of sight. "Where are we going?"

The driver glanced at him through the corner of the mirror. "Shortcut...you see." The car came to a sudden stop. Before David could say a word, the door opposite him flew open and the barrel of a silencer stared him in the face. David recognized the man behind the gun but didn't let him know it, the man in the waiting room hiding behind the newspaper.

"Hand your gun over...very slowly," the man in a heavy brown overcoat demanded.

The driver saw the gun in the reflection of his rearview mirror. "No trouble…where is money?"

The man took David's gun and slid it under his belt. He quickly turned his gun to the back of the driver's head, squeezing a quick decisive round, then quickly turned back on David. The bullet passed through the driver's brain, shattering the windshield upon its exit. Blood was splattered over the cracked glass, with pieces of flesh and brain oozing down the glass like an army of red snails sliding across a sidewalk.

With his right hand keeping the gun on David, the man reached over the seat with his left, grabbing the dead driver's shoulder and pulling his body back into the seat. He then reached into the corpse's shirt pocket, retrieving the five one hundred dollar bills he gave him earlier. The man wiped the corpse's blood from his hand onto the back of the front seat.

"What do you want?" David asked. "I'm not carrying much money."

"Shut your face!" the man yelled.

Suddenly David's door flew open, with several gigantic paws yanking him out of the cab. Two men, who seemed to David as tall as skyscrapers, wide as houses, and thick as tanks, held him against the outside of the cab. Both men were extremely muscle bound, with ink creeping out past their shirt collars. They held David by each of his arms like a vise. They did a quick pat down, uncovering some change, a wallet, penlight, and ink pen. One handed the wallet to the man in the overcoat, releasing the rest to fall to the pavement.

Chapter 23

Then one of the brutes spotted a silver chain against David's neck. He ran his hand down the front of David's collar, pulling out the crimson key. The silver chain snapped and the man handed the broken necklace to the man in the overcoat. He stared at the crimson key, holding it up into the dim light by its chain. "What is this?"

David stared at the key, his mind grasping for an explanation. "It's my girlfriend's key."

The man glared into David's eyes as he shook his head slowly. Then he whipped the chain around and slung the crimson key through the air. David's eyes filled with desperation as he watched the key float in and out of sight through the dimly lit alley, and possibly all hopes of finding out what really happened to his mother. Just before he could see where the crimson key would come to rest, his eyes entered a blurred darkness. Pain shattered his face from a blow to his jaw. The bitter cold wind whipped mercilessly through the alley, but David did not feel its sting, only the sting of another fist to his jaw. His interrogator fixed his eyes on him, those evil black eyes cutting a hole right through him. "You know what I want," the man said in an evil tone.

David did not answer but only met his stare. A sudden blow to the ribs sent pain shooting through David's body. Then before he could breathe, a matching blow from the other side rocked his entire body. "I want the name of who you are working for," the man in the overcoat demanded.

David realized he was in the midst of a dire situation. This man before him would kill him no matter what answer he gave. The truth would get him killed, and so would a lie. So he played the dumb card. "What are you talking about? You have me mistaken…" He didn't get a chance to finish the sentence. A sharp blow to his jaw shut him up, a left hook from the man in the overcoat.

"You seem to be brighter than that," the man said. "I don't have time to play games, so tell me what I want."

David turned his head slowly back to the man, feeling the blood trickling from the corner of his mouth. He returned the man's stare, taking notice of his own gun in the man's belt. "You are right," David said, then hesitated. "I'm not dumb…but what choice do I have? If I give you an answer…then you will kill me. So give me some reasonable options."

The man smiled a wide evil smile. "I don't know about reasonable, but I can give you options." He leaned closer. "I have ways to make you talk…and eventually you will beg me to kill you." David felt the pressure of the barrel on his left knee. "Let's say we start here."

With all his might, David buried his right knee into the man's groin. The man instantly doubled over in pain. The gun in his hand released, falling down to the pavement and bouncing out of sight underneath the taxi, while the gun in his belt fell into some nearby trash on the ground. David spotted the handle of his gun not far from his right foot. He suddenly dropped his weight, freeing himself from the gigantic men's grip. Hitting the pavement on his knees, he desperately reached for his gun. Within an inch of it, he was suddenly slung back against the body of the taxi. Body blows from both sides rocked David and the car as well. The man in the overcoat groaned as he attempted to straighten up, his evil black eyes filled with rage.

Then David heard a click and saw a reflection of light from the shiny blade of a knife. He swung a foot at the glimmering blade but came up inches short. The man lunged at David, falling against him hard while burying the blade into David's left thigh. Immense pain shot through David's leg, causing him to yell out. The man with his weight against David laughed. "I should have cut your balls off…and I will if you don't start talking."

"First you tell me who you are working for," David said, as he felt warm blood running down his leg.

The man still had his hand securely on the knife. As he stared into David's eyes, he twisted the blade slightly. David felt the blade scrape the bone and yelled from the excruciating pain, almost to the point of passing out. Then there came an echo though the alley of two men yelling. David caught a glimpse out the corner of his eye. Two flashlights bobbled as two policemen came running. The man pulled the blade out of David's leg, sending another wave of pain throughout his body. The men fled, letting David drop to the cold wet pavement. David hit the ground hard, grabbing his pain-riddled thigh, rolling face first into wet slush. He rolled over on his back as his clothes soaked up the icy cold water. With his eyes shut from the pain, he felt a warm sensation on his cheeks. He slowly opened his eyes directly into the bright beam of the policeman's flashlight, the last thing he remembered before awakening in the hospital.

Chapter 24

David woke in the hospital feeling no pain at all. The pain medication had him floating on air. Several strange faces lingered about him, and one familiar face too—Lieutenant Jacoby, Moreno's boss. His stare was strong and constant as he stepped closer to the bed. "You are a lucky man."

David smiled a long while, due to the medication. Jacoby shook his head. "Can you tell me what happened?"

David attempted to sit up in bed. A snippet of pain overtook the medication, reviving his drugged memory. He quickly grabbed his thigh, feeling the thick bandage, as the events flashed through his mind. "I got into a cab here," he slowly said. "I instructed the driver to take me to the hotel. On the way, he turned down an alley. He said it was a shortcut. Then he stopped quickly and I was staring down the barrel of a gun. The man turned quickly, popping the driver in the back of his head. Then two gorillas pulled me out the door and ruffed me up. I managed to land my knee up in the man's groin… but later paid for it with a knife in my leg."

"After you come down from this medication, we will need a good description of these three men." Jacoby hesitated. "Meanwhile…you are off this case. Moreno filled me in on everything that has happened. I am reopening this case. The gun we found under the taxi matches the one used to kill the cleaning lady. He was definitely after you. I will be putting several detectives on this case first thing in the morning." He paused. "But I have to tell you, there is not a lot to go on. What leads do you have?"

David looked around. "Where is my notebook?"

Jacoby pulled open the drawer of the nightstand and grabbed the notebook. David took it and flipped through the pages. He stopped on a page with six names on it, the other models that worked with Amber. He tore out the page and handed it to Jacoby. "Unfortunately this is all I have. These were the other models working with Amber Paige at the time. All other leads have led to dead ends."

Jacoby took the page, folded it, and stuffed it into his pocket. "You get some rest… I will personally see to this case, and will keep you informed." He then turned to the door.

"Lieutenant," David said, just as he opened the door. "Has the crime scene investigation been completed?"

"Yes, just before I came here."

"Did they find a crimson-colored key on a silver chain?" David asked with hope in his eyes.

Jacoby gave David a confused stare. "No…is it of any importance?"

David lay back, his eyes floating to the ceiling. "No…of no importance." David closed his eyes as he heard Jacoby exit. Thoughts of the letter his mother left flowed through his mind; the crimson key held the secret to his biological mother's demise. Though under the influence of pain medication, he still felt the anguish knowing that he may never find out what actually happened to her.

Then his cell came to life inside the nightstand drawer, vibrating and buzzing like a bumble bee trapped inside a box. David cracked open the drawer, then fumbled around within until his hand landed on the jittering bug. A quick glance at the caller id revealed it was from South Carolina, Kimberly. David answered and filled her in on all the details, except for one—Sheridan. He told her that he was off the case and it had been reopened by the police department. He also told her about the key being lost and his fear they would never know what actually happened to Amber. She then asked when he would be home. He hesitated, as thoughts of Sheridan in the mountains rushed through his mind. He answered with uncertainty, explaining to her that he had agreed to check into another missing person case for a friend. They eventually said their goodnights, and David lay in heavy thought. A guilty feeling rushed in, as thoughts of Sheridan plagued his mind. Though he reasoned with himself, he still could not shake the feeling of guilt. He and Kimberly were very close, and had been forever, but there was no commitment between them, so why this feeling of remorse? Could it be that Kimberly meant more to him than he realized or was able to admit?

David's hand began to tingle, breaking his train of thought. He pulled the trembling phone close to his face. Sheridan beckoned. "Well hello there," David answered in a drunken state.

"David? Have you been drinking?" Sheridan questioned.

"Nope...don't need to."

Sheridan gave a little laugh. "What are you up to?"

"Just chilling...here in the hospital, they are giving me the good stuff."

"What!" Sheridan's voice filled with shock, and then she began to fire questions. "What happened? Are you okay? What room are you in?"

"Slow down," he cut her off. "I will be fine. I got stabbed in my leg, and you can't come here. It's not safe. The man is still out there, and I don't want you involved."

"I am already involved."

"You know what I mean," he answered. "This man or the one who hired him is probably watching the hospital and maybe this room. He was here following me when I visited Moreno. So you have to stay clear... just for a while. Lieutenant Jacoby has reopened the case and is personally taking it over. So this should wrap up in a day or two."

"Okay then," she said reluctantly. "So when can I see you?"

David suddenly remembered the date he had planned for tomorrow night. "This really sucks. I had a special date set up for tomorrow night. I had planned on you waiting for me at Central Park, and then surprising you when I came up in a horse and carriage."

"Oh," she sighed.

"A romantic carriage ride through Central Park, under the stars."

"That is so sweet," she remarked. "How did you know that I loved carriage rides?"

David thought. "I just felt that you would. We have only known each other for a short period, but I feel as if we are connected."

"I feel it too…and it scares me."

There was a silent moment between them.

"I have an idea," Sheridan said. "Since you had such a sweet date planned, I think we should plan another trip to the mountains this weekend."

"That sounds great. But I don't think I will be able to ride a snowmobile… And I definitely won't be able to ski."

"Snowmobiling and skiing are the furthest things from my mind."

Chapter 25

The next morning David was forced out of bed by the nurses and a determined physical therapist. He painfully made his way out of the bed and down the hall with the assistance of crutches, tiring very easily. On his way back up the hallway, David spotted a familiar face. Moreno presented a painful smile. "Sorry I wasn't there to block that knife for you."

David strained a laugh. "That would have been mighty nice of you. Did you bring doughnuts?"

Moreno shook his head. "Maybe tomorrow—I should be released."

"Won't be any need—I will be out of here tomorrow myself," David said as he glanced at the physical therapist, a thick black woman matching his height.

The black woman smiled while she shook her head. "If you keep progressing, then after one more day. Thursday you may leave."

They made it back to David's room and he flopped back into bed. Moreno pulled a chair closer to the bed and sat down. "Are you happy that your case has been reopened?"

"In a way," David answered as concern filled his face. "I'm afraid that they will continue hitting dead ends and I will never find out what happened to my real mother, especially now."

Moreno's eyes narrowed in confusion. "What do you mean especially now?"

"The crimson key is lost. It was supposed to unlock the mystery of my mother's disappearance. The man ripped it from my neck and tossed it down the alley. I did not see exactly where it landed. And the CSI team did not find it."

"Did you give Jacoby the list of names?"

David ran his fingers through his hair as concern still shadowed his face. "Yes...and those are the only leads we have."

"Jacoby said he would take care of this case personally. I guarantee that he will throw several detectives on that list today. I bet that you will have answers by late today."

David stared out his door emotionless as nurses passed by. "I sure hope you are right. But I have a bad feeling about this."

Later that afternoon a call to the police department was placed. A pedestrian reported seeing an object resembling a body that had washed up beneath the Williamsburg Bridge over the East River. The area was suddenly flooded with men in blue, including Lieutenant Jacoby. A CSI team was assembled and at the scene promptly. The body was fished from the edge of the icy waters, a middle-aged man in a heavy brown overcoat. The air had a stagnant smell to it, not from the corpse but from the filthy water. The cause of death was quickly determined—not from drowning but from a bullet that had pierced his overcoat and lodged in his chest. The body had been in the water for only twelve hours or less. Fresh blood drenched the front of his overcoat, with an older stain on his pants along his right thigh. There wasn't any identification found on the body—just a knife with partially dried blood on it. The CSI team took prints, and then placed the body into a body bag to be delivered to the medical examiner.

About 5 p.m., David's phone jiggled to life. He lifted the phone and eyed the caller ID. His face lit up upon recognition of the number. "Hello Darling."

"You sure do sound a lot better than you did last night," Sheridan said.

"Just the sound of your voice brings me to life."

Sheridan chuckled. "You must still be on the good stuff."

"Maybe just a little," he replied. "But hopefully I will be out of here tomorrow. I sure would like to see you, but I don't want to put you in any danger."

"You haven't heard anything on your case?"

"Not a word," David answered as he sat up in bed. "I was hoping they would have caught the guy by now. That way I could sneak you in for a visit."

"That would have been sweet. But now you will have to wait until Saturday."

Disappointment filled David's face. "What happened to Thursday and Friday?"

Sheridan hesitated. "I will be out of town. I have to fly out to Buffalo first thing in the morning. A friend from college asked me to represent her in a case. The trial is Friday morning and I will be flying back later that evening."

"What in the world am I going to do for two days without you and a case to work on?"

"Rest," Sheridan replied. "That is what the doctor ordered, didn't he?"

David sighed. "I guess so...but I'm not used to resting that much."

"Believe me," she said and paused. "You will definitely need the rest for this weekend... And that is a promise."

Chapter 26

Bored to death, David stared at the clock, 8:30 p.m. He had channeled surfed through an ocean of television shows with not a one interesting him. Even the golf channel was nothing but an infomercial. Just then a smiling face appeared in the doorway. Moreno walked in dressed in street clothes. David smiled as he noticed a familiar bag in his hand. "That had better be what I think it is."

Moreno returned his smile. "You better believe it." He handed the bag to David. "Cream-filled just like you like."

David looked up at Moreno. "There seems to be some regular doughnuts in here too."

"Well I'll be damn," Moreno said, pretending to be shocked. "I guess I will have to take them back." Then he smiled.

David took a bite. "Mmmm…I never realized just how good these were."

Moreno joined in. "Hospital food has a way of bringing out the great taste of real food. Did you catch the local news at six?"

David wiped his mouth. "No I didn't. Why?"

"They fished a body out of the East River today, a middle-aged man wearing a heavy brown overcoat."

David's eyes met Moreno's. "You gotta be kidding."

"Afraid not…You think it may be your man?"

David shook his head slowly. "I don't know, but it does match my description." He paused. "Did they give a name?"

"No," Moreno replied, snatching another victim from the bag. "John Doe was the name they gave because there wasn't any identification on him."

"William Nelson," Lieutenant Jacoby said, walking through the door. "We matched up his prints in the system." Jacoby stared at the two devouring their doughnuts. "Any extra?"

David handed him the bag. "Sure, help yourself." Then his eyes met Jacoby's. "Is this my guy?"

Jacoby took a bite. "His prints matched the prints on the gun under the taxi. And the bullet we took from the cleaning lady matched the gun as well."

"So that wraps up the case on her," Moreno remarked.

"They are falling like dominos," Jacoby remarked. "The case on Scully has closed because Sullivan's blood and partial prints were at the scene. The Sullivan case is now closed because Nelson's fingerprints were found on the wiring of the bomb. And now it brings us to the Amber Paige case, which is finally ready for closure."

David's eyes narrowed as a sudden burst of anger filled his soul. "What do you mean closure? We haven't found Amber yet."

"Now just hear me out," Jacoby responded to David's outburst. "We have reason to believe that Nelson was involved in this twenty-five years ago. At that time he was very big into gambling and organized crime."

"He is a little too young. And what has that got to do with Amber Paige?" David asked.

"Nelson is 55. And it turns out that Nelson's sister was a model for the same agency then. And he was known to fool around with many of the models at that time." Jacoby pulled out his notes. "He served time in the nineties for second degree murder of another model. So we feel he probably killed Amber Paige because she was pregnant with his child, and he was already married."

David stared at the ceiling, thinking to himself. "Can this scumbag be my father? I can come out with the truth now about who I really am, and ask for a DNA test. No…I had rather not know than to find out that this is my father." David lowered his gaze. "What about the names I gave you?"

Jacoby referred to his notes. "Three of those names perished in the 9/11 attacks. One died from cancer a year ago. One committed suicide ten years ago. And the other was in a boating accident fifteen years ago and lost at sea. The apartment where Miss Paige was living burned down in the spring of 1987. Everyone that owned or worked at that modeling agency at that time is either dead or missing." He paused. "William

Nelson was the final piece of the puzzle. And most assuredly he murdered Amber Paige and disposed of her body somehow."

David's face crinkled as he reasoned with the facts. Jacoby glanced at Moreno, then back at David. "So…if you don't have any other evidence, then I think I need to close this case once and for all."

"Who murdered Nelson?" Moreno asked.

"No one," Jacoby answered. "The wound was self-inflicted."

David continued to gaze off in thought. Jacoby stared into David's opened eyes. "Do you have something more to say?"

David focused on Jacoby's stare. "No…close it."

Jacoby rose, giving David his hand. David took his hand. "It's been a pleasure working with you," Jacoby said with a smile as they shook hands.

"The pleasure is all mine," David said with an unsettled look on his face. Then he watched Jacoby leave.

"You don't seem happy with the outcome of your case," Moreno remarked.

David turned his focus to Moreno, who was polishing off the last doughnut. "I have that strange feeling again. Something just doesn't feel right about this. I can see how the evidence points to the same conclusion. But I just don't think it feels right. And who commits suicide by shooting himself in the chest?"

"So what are you going to do about it?"

David shook his head. "I guess I will have to live with it. All the witnesses and evidence are gone."

"So when will you be heading back to South Carolina?"

A smile grew on David's face. "I have some politicking to deal with this weekend."

Moreno laughed. "You don't appear to be in any shape for much politicking."

"That is what I told her," David remarked. "But she still insisted on carrying me to the mountains this weekend."

"Gee, I can picture it now, you on crutches off in the mountains alone with a beautiful woman. And she is waiting on you hand and foot to make sure that you are comfortable while she nurses you back to health." Moreno added while laughing under his breath, "Are you sure you're up to the task?"

David grinned. "Someone has got to make the sacrifice."

They both laughed out loud.

Chapter 27

David tossed and turned, not able to sleep. He glanced at the clock, 1:15 a.m. He could remember every twenty-minute interval for the past three hours. Every time he rolled over facing the clock twenty minutes had passed. Finally he surrendered and rose out of bed just as a night nurse was coming in to check on him. "And where do you think you are going?"

David smiled at the young nurse, intrigued by her strawberry-colored hair and her captivating eyes. "I think I will run out for some pizza…you want some?"

She laughed. "Do you need something to help you sleep?"

"Do you serve alcohol?"

She shook her head as she walked back out the door. "I'll be right back."

David did not stick around, hobbling out the door just as she went out of sight. He made the turn down the hall without getting caught. Figuring he must be safe, he slowed his pace. He traveled the desolate hallway until he reached the elevator. Across from the elevator was a sitting area in front of a large window overlooking the parking lot on the south end of the hospital. He approached the window as if summoned to look outside. David stared out into the cold dark night, while random snowflakes danced their way to the frozen tundra below. Then a strange sight drew his attention to his left. Down below on the frozen sidewalk stood a woman in a low-cut red dress, her cleavage and bare skin on her chest very visible. David moved closer to the window for a clearer view. "She has got to be freezing," he thought to himself. "Why isn't she wearing a coat? Why doesn't someone help her inside where it is warm?" The woman was looking down at her chest as she felt around with her hands, as if searching for something. Her long blonde hair draped over, blanketing most of her face. Then the woman suddenly looked up directly at David. Their eyes connected as shock filled his face. She resembled his mother Amber, but he could not be sure from this distance and the poor lighting where she stood. She was wearing a dress similar to the dress Amber wore in his dream at the house in the mountains with Sheridan.

"There you are," the young nurse said. The sudden sound of her voice startled David, causing him to jump as he turned to her. He quickly turned his head back, but the vision was gone. "What are you looking at?" she asked, staring out the window.

David swept his eyes from left to right. "Just watching it snow."

"Did you see someone wearing red?"

David jerked his head in her direction, eyes locked instantly while thinking to himself, "She saw her too."

The nurse smiled. "Santa Claus?"

Disappointed and not amused, David squeezed out a smile. "Looked like Little Red Riding Hood to me."

She chuckled as she helped him back to the room. David took his medication but continued to struggle, contemplating his apparition. "There is no such thing as ghosts," he thought to himself. "But what did I see? Or is it just the medication causing hallucinations? That has to be it. Anyway, the case is solved and now closed."

David wrestled with his thoughts and the medication as well. The medication tugged at his eyelids, as if weights hung from his lashes. Finally the medication won the battle as he dropped into a profound slumber. He was in such a profound sleep that the nurse returned an hour later, taking his vitals without him even knowing it. When he opened his eyes he was in the ally where he was stabbed. Just like the dream before, he watched himself as if in an outer body experience. Only this time he watched himself in a real life event. The dream seemed so real to him—he felt the bitter cold air whipping through the alley, and the stench of rotten food lingered in the air just as he remembered.

The cab came to a stop in the alley as he visualized in his head time and time again. David watched as his presumed father appeared from the shadows, diving into the cab with a gun drawn. His heart leaped in his chest just as it had done then. David witnessed once again his father turning the gun to the back of the driver's head. In an instant, blood sprayed the windshield and dash as the bullet shattered the glass. The taste of death lingered on David's lips just as it did then. He then felt the sudden tug of the two huge men as they yanked him out of the taxi. He felt once again the pain from the blows to his ribs as the two men pounded his body.

David watched his father creep around the taxi, then stare at him eye to eye with his evil black eyes, not realizing he was staring into his son's face. If he had, then David would not be alive to have this dream. David watched carefully as his father held up the necklace, the dangling key glowing in the dim light. Then he watched his father toss the crimson key down the alley. The necklace floated in slow motion like a feather, finally coming to rest on an old wooden crate. David saw what he couldn't see that night. An untimely slap to his face pulled his vision away from the necklace, but now he knew where the key came to rest. He wondered why the police failed to collect the key when working the crime scene.

David turned his attention back to the taxi. A tiny glimmer of light caught his eye—the reflection from the shiny blade of a knife. His heart leaped as he watched his father drive the knife into his thigh. The immense pain shot through his body just as it did then. The sudden pain caused David to scream out loud as he quickly rose in bed, drenched in sweat.

Chapter 28

Two nurses barreled into David's room. "Mr. Peoples, are you okay?" one asked, as the other silenced the beeping monitor. "Your pulse rate just spiked. You were on the verge of a massive coronary."

David wiped the sweat from his brow. "I guess I was dreaming."

"Dreaming," the nurse remarked. "That had to have been one hell of a nightmare."

David slowly lowered himself to the bed as pictures from his nightmare ran circles in his head. He recalled every painful detail. "Why is finding this key now so important?" he thought to himself. "The case has been solved." He thought for a minute. "This necklace is the only personal item I have that belonged to my real mother. I don't even have a picture of her. Maybe that is it. That's why it is weighing so heavily on my mind. And that is where these dreams are coming from. I need to find the crimson key so I will have a personal possession of my mother's."

David drifted back to sleep. The nurse checked in on him and found him resting peacefully, or so she thought. She smiled, then continued on her rounds. David's eyes suddenly darted left then right behind closed eyelids. His hands and arms twitched. He had passed reality and was sinking into dreamland once again. This dream began as a good dream. David watched himself being released from the hospital as he stepped outside into the cold air. He could actually feel the sting of the air against his cheeks as he hailed a cab. A new snow blanketed the ground an inch or so deep. He was instantly enticed by an overwhelming aroma of cooked bacon. He could almost taste it, making his mouth water and stomach cry as he watched people across the street filing into a busy diner. A cab pulled to the curb, slinging snow and slush onto David's shoes. He stomped his feet and then opened the door. Taking one last draw from the bacon-filled air, he threw his crutches in first and fell in behind.

David watched himself as he gazed through the side window at the people of Manhattan as they went on their busy way. Most carried briefcases and wore tailored suits. Others wore mismatched clothes and shoes, with florescent highlighted hairdos. David's attention was drawn to a thin lanky lady being dragged by six dogs on leashes. In passing, he glimpsed something in bright red. He quickly leaned back to catch another glimpse through the grimy rear window. There at the entrance of an alley stood a beautiful blonde lady in a red dress.

It was his mother Amber as he remembered her from his dream in the mountains, wearing the same low-cut dress. The alley behind her looked similar to the one that David was stabbed in. As in his vision earlier she did not wear a coat, only the low-cut red dress. Her long blonde hair waved in the breeze, like the tail of a horse in full stride.

David yelled for the driver to stop. By the time the cab pulled to a curb, they were over a block away. David quickly paid the fare and hobbled back up the sidewalk in her direction. He watched himself as he maneuvered through the unwavering crowd, no one taking notice of his desperation. He could still see Amber up ahead with an impatient look on her face as she glanced repeatedly back and forth between him and up the alley. A squeaking sound became present, growing louder very rapidly. Only David heard the irritating noise, not the others nearby. He began grimacing as it began to hurt his ears.

David saw his mother, Amber up ahead kneel down and write something in the snow with her long white finger. He quickened his pace as he could see fear in her eyes. The squeaking noise became unbearable, causing him to stop and cover his ears, letting his crutches fall to the ground. Amber stood up again only about a hundred feet from him, overwhelmed with desperation. With a fear-drenched face, she held her arms to him. Urgency forced him to continue, limping painfully to her while keeping his hands over his ears. Then Amber was sucked down the alley, her spirit stretched as she held her arms to him.

The squeaking noise stopped abruptly as she vanished into the alley. Out of breath, tired from his struggle, David reached the alley and peered down the vacant passage. The only thing visible was a dark wide figure standing at the far end, covered in shadow from a corner building. David could not make out a face from this distance. Then something on its face glimmered in the narrow sunlight. It gleamed gold and blinded him; he had to guard his eyes. He turned his head from the glare, as his eyes fell upon Amber's writing in the snow. Only one word: RUBY. He then looked back down the alley, finding that the strange image had faded away.

Chapter 29

David felt his arm being squeezed tight, like in a vise. He opened his eyes to bright strawberry hair. The nurse was taking his blood pressure. She noticed his stare. "Sorry if I woke you. Were you dreaming again?"

David rubbed his face with his free hand. "Yes…I think so."

She planted the cold stethoscope on his warm bare chest. "I thought so. Your heart rate elevated. But not nearly as much as the last one."

David glanced at the clock, 5:42 a.m. "I might as well get up now. Breakfast will be here in about a half hour. I sure do have a taste for bacon."

She grinned. "I doubt if there will be any bacon on your tray. But you should be out by lunch time. The diner across the street serves a great BLT."

"So I am free to go."

"No," she replied. "I am not the doctor. He will be in to see you after breakfast."

David opened the morning paper. He thumbed through the paper until he stumbled upon a particular article. The article was titled: Open and Shut Case on a Missing Model from 1986. A frown inched across his face as he read the article. The reporter stated that the 25-year-old case was reopened and shut in record time. It went on to say that all the evidence of Amber Paige's disappearance pointed to an affair she had then with William Nelson. He was the only missing link in the case, but not anymore. His body was found floating in the East River after an apparent suicide. Even without a body, the police were confident that he murdered Amber Paige and disposed of the body. Without any other evidence to go on, the case has been closed for good. David knew that the article was accurate and the writing was on the wall, but he hated the outcome of it all.

Later, after a disappointing breakfast free of taste, David wandered to the window, staring out at the snow-capped building tops. His phone tap danced on the nightstand. He first glanced at the clock, 8:05 a.m. David limped to the stand, saving the phone just as it dived off the edge. He quickly answered without checking the caller id. A sweet but tired voice spoke from miles away. "David," Kimberly said with a drained voice. "How are you feeling this morning?"

David smiled. "Better...it's good to hear your voice. Are you at work?"

She sighed. "No...I had to pull an all-nighter last night. I just got home. I thought I would give you a call before crashing."

"I should be getting out of here today."

"That's great news," she responded. "How is your case coming along?"

"Been solved. The police wrapped it all up in one day."

"So," Kimberly said slowly, then hesitated. "You have found your father."

"Unfortunately," he replied with apparent anger, "he was the man who stabbed me. As far as I'm concerned, he never existed."

"That's understandable… Did he know who you really are?"

David hesitated. "No," he said and paused. "He stared me right into my eyes. I felt the cold stare of an evil man, not the warmth of a father's gaze."

A silent moment passed. "So how did the key help you find him?"

"It didn't," he answered. "The key was lost. It was jerked from my neck and thrown down the alley. He raised it up and stared at it for a while. I'm not sure, but I think he recognized it." David sighed. "Anyway…the case was solved without it."

A silent moment passed. "But where is Amber?"

"We will never know," David replied sadly. "The key was supposed to reveal the man responsible. And we already know it was William Nelson. And with him dead, so died the secret. The key could not have told us where she is. She couldn't have known ahead of time where she was to be buried."

"That's right," Kimberly replied, then paused. "It's still a shame that the key is lost. It is the only thing you had that belonged to her. You don't even have a picture of her. You don't even know what she looked like."

The phone fell silent. "I believe I do."

"How is that possible?" Kimberly asked. "You only have the physical description from Alice."

The phone fell silent again. "Do you believe in ghosts?"

"As long as we have known one another," she responded, "we have never had this discussion."

"Well?"

She hesitated. "There have been several occasions when I saw Dad."

David could hear the emotion in her voice. "You never told me this before."

"I didn't want you to think I was crazy," she said in a shaky voice. "Have you seen Amber?"

"In dreams, not in real life." He paused and remembered. "Except once maybe…last night I thought I saw her standing outside looking up at me. But it was too dark to tell for sure."

"I don't know what to tell you. My faith…well, we don't believe in ghosts. But there is a part of me that doesn't rule out the possibility. Maybe if there is a very important reason, God may use spirits to lead us in the right direction." Kimberly paused. "What is she doing in these dreams?"

David stood and walked to the window, separating the blinds with his fingers, peeking through. "I think she is trying to help me find the key. But why? The case has been solved."

"Maybe it still answers the mystery to why she was murdered," she replied. "But then maybe again she just wants you to find it so you will have a personal belonging of hers." Kimberly paused. The only sound on the phone was their breathing. "I can't tell you what to do or what to believe. But if it were me…I would not ignore it. This may be the last chance ever to find out what really happened to your mother…and solve this mystery. If you don't, she may haunt your dreams forever."

Chapter 30

David was released just before noon just as the strawberry-haired nurse had said. The sky was thick and completely gray; not a hint of sun peeked through anywhere. A blanket of freshly fallen snow about an inch thick covered the ground and building tops. He exited the front doors on crutches. The bitter breeze nipped at his cheeks and any crack it could seep through. David didn't seem to mind the freezing breeze today. That is because the enticing aroma of fresh-cooked bacon rode the wind. He could almost taste it, making his mouth water and stomach cry. He remembered what the strawberry-haired nurse had told him about the great BLTs in the diner across the street. As he hailed a cab he watched people filing into the diner. Just then he felt weight on his feet. Looking down, he saw snow and slush where his feet should have been. He stomped the slush off his shoes, took one last draw of the bacon-filled air, then opened the door to the cab and threw his crutches in first before falling inside. Unaware to him at this point, the events were unfolding just as they had in his dream.

David watched the people of Manhattan as he passed by, people of different nationalities as well as dress. He then took particular notice of a woman being dragged by six dogs. This triggered his memory of the dream. He stared out the side window with a puzzled face. Suddenly he remembered exactly how the dream unfolded. He jerked his head back and peered through the grimy rear window. All he could make out was something in bright red. A vivid picture of Amber lingered in his thoughts.

David told the cab driver to stop. He was well past the alley when he exited the cab, just like in his dream. He stretched his neck upward to get a glimpse of Amber at the entrance to the alley where he was stabbed. The crowd was thick, not releasing any images past fifty feet or so. David felt his heart race with anticipation. He began maneuvering his way through the immense crowd. Everyone stared at David on his crutches as he made his way towards the alley. He kept a constant watch up ahead, ignoring the stares, to see if Amber was going to appear to him as she did in his dream.

A glimpse of something red trickled through the crowd. David quickened his pace in excitement. The relentless crowd relinquished not an ounce of pity for this crippled man. They cursed under their breaths as David accidently bumped several when passing. He could still catch a glimpse of something red ahead, but could not make out Amber's spirit yet. Just then, David's right crutch lost traction on a piece of ice. His world turned upside down as he crashed to the sidewalk. A familiar sharp pain flared from his thigh.

Before trying to get to his feet, David peered through the legs up ahead in hopes of seeing Amber waiting for him at the alley. The bright red image he had been glimpsing appeared in plain sight now. Disappointment displaced his excitement. Up ahead were three teenagers talking, one wearing a bright red coat. David then noticed a dark hand reaching down to him, a hand connected to a dark blue uniform. He looked up into the eyes of a policeman as he took the hand. He was African American with broad shoulders and a powerful grip. The policeman smiled a wide smile as he pulled David to his feet, then reached down and retrieved the crutches. David took notice right away that one of his teeth was capped with gold. He remembered something gold flashing from the face of the dark wide figure in the alley. Maybe this was it, he thought, even though he had not fallen in his dream.

"Are you all right?" the policeman asked.

David smiled. "Just hurt my pride a bit—that's all I hope."

The policeman brushed some dirt and snow from David's back. "Where are you headed?"

"Back to my hotel," David replied. "I stopped the cab because I thought I saw someone I knew. But I see now that I was mistaken."

"Do you want me to catch you a cab?"

David noticed they were in front of a café. "No thank you…I think I will go inside for a cup of coffee and rest a bit. These sticks will wear you down," he said as he held up the crutches.

The policeman smiled. "You are right about that. I had to use them once for about two weeks."

"Thank you again for your help," David said. "May I buy you a cup of coffee?"

"No thank you. I must be on my way."

David watched the policeman disappear in the crowd. He then turned, facing the café. The outside was all in red. David took notice of the sign above the door: The Ruby Red Café. He smiled as he remembered his dream. This must be the RUBY Amber wrote in the snow, he thought. But what does it all mean? And why didn't he remember falling in the dream? David dismissed his thoughts and entered the café, hoping they had a BLT on the menu.

Chapter 31

Quaint and small, the Ruby Red Café had an ambiance like the world class restaurants of New York City, but without the price. What the menu lacked it made up for it with taste. The crowded dining area was a testament to its great food. David entered and took the last available table at the rear. Before his seat could get warm, a bubbly petite brunette waited on him. He ordered a hot coffee to warm his bones while he studied the menu.

David drifted off in thought as he looked at the menu. The dream weighed heavily on his mind. He couldn't figure out what it all meant. Playing back the dream in his thoughts, he tried to figure out what each event represented. Amber standing at the alley must mean that he needed to be here for a reason, to find the key no doubt. The word RUBY that she wrote in the snow must be this café, of course. Maybe someone here found the necklace and is wearing it now. David took notice of everyone in the café and what they were wearing around their necks.

"Are you looking for someone?" a voice asked.

David looked to the voice, the petite waitress. "No, not really."

"Are you ready to order?"

"I guess," David replied, and then noticed a silver chain around her neck. The chain had a knot tied in it as if it had been broken. The other end was hidden beneath her waitress outfit. He stared at her neck in deep thought.

"Are you okay?" she asked.

"Did you break your necklace?"

She put a hand to her neck. "It was broken when I found it. But it was so beautiful that I wanted to wear it anyway. I will eventually replace the chain."

David felt his heart beating, anticipating the discovery of the lost crimson key and the hopes of finding his mother. "May I see it?"

The waitress reached behind her neck. "Why of course," she said as she pulled the chain over her head. She raised her hand, pulling out the entire necklace. "Isn't it beautiful?"

David stared at the necklace, his heart returning to normal. "That is a very beautiful cameo you got there." Disappointed, he ordered the special of the day, not even knowing what it may be. His thoughts returned to his dream. Everything in his dream was accounted for, except for the loud squeaking noise. David rose and went to the restroom. After his business, he went to the old rustic sink to wash up. The plumbing appeared to be twenty years old. When he turned the faucet on for hot water, the pipes squealed from vibration, similar to the sound he heard in his dream. David returned to his seat even more confused than he was before. Nothing made sense, nothing fit. And where is the crimson key? Amber in the red dress brought him to this place. Except the red dress was really the teen in a red coat. The golden glare from a dark wide figure was the policeman's gold-capped tooth. He helped him to his feet after the fall. Amber writing the word RUBY in the snow had to mean The Ruby Red Café. The loud squeaking noise came from the old pipes. His thoughts raced as he picked at his food. What does all this mean? What was he missing?

As David stared down at his plate in deep thought, a feeling swept over him, an awkward feeling that someone was watching him. He raised his head, finding no one. Then out of the corner of his eye he caught a glimpse of red. Just outside the large front window was someone in a red dress staring in at him. Just then a couple walked past David to the checkout counter, momentarily blocking his view. After they had passed, the lady in the window had disappeared.

David quickly jumped to his feet to get a better look. Still no one was there anymore.

"Is something wrong?" the waitress asked as she approached.

David pulled out two twenty-dollar bills and handed them to her. "The food was great. I have to run. Keep the change."

She watched him curiously as he hustled out the door.

Chapter 32

David rushed out the café and around the corner as fast as his crutches would carry him. He did not see Amber anywhere, but just seeing the apparition gave him new strength. Maybe now something from his dream would come together and make sense. David made his way to the alley. He stood at one end and stared to the other. Amber was nowhere to be seen, nor the dark figure in his dream. Minutes passed as he stood wondering what to do next. The alley gave him an eerie feeling. Though it was dimly lit when he got stabbed, he still recognized its surroundings. He slowly walked through it, stopping and looking around occasionally, as if expecting to see another apparition. The bitter cold wind howled through the alley, making his eyes water.

David stopped at the place where he was stabbed. He relived the event in his mind. Snow had blanketed the scene, but he recognized every detail of the area from memory. He tried to imagine where the necklace could have come to rest, picturing it floating in mid-air just before his sight was blurred from a blow to his jaw. He remembered the earlier dream in which the necklace came to rest on a wooden crate. With a good idea where it could have landed, he began to use the rubber ends of the crutches to sweep away the snow. All other thoughts lifted from his mind as he searched diligently.

A homeless lady pushing a rusting shopping cart approached the opening at the far end of the alley. The wheels squeaked as she rolled along. She stopped and stared at David for a minute. David glanced up at her, not recognizing what she was at first. Her image to him was dark and wide with the shadow from the building covering her face. He thought nothing of her as he continued with his search. Thinking nothing of him either, she went on her way, squeaking down the sidewalk. The squeaking sound caught David's attention. He began to think as the squeaking sound registered in his brain. Then her dark figure at the end of the alley triggered a thought. David hobbled quickly in her direction. As he turned the corner, he yelled for her to stop. Frightened by his approach, she quickened her pace.

When the homeless lady attempted to make the next turn, the shopping cart overturned, spilling out her prized possessions. Frantically she set the cart upright and began to pick up her things. David closed in fast. After realizing she was caught, the homeless lady took up a cane for her defense. As David approached, she attacked, swinging desperately at him. He had to quickly raise a crutch to block the blows from the cane. "Stop! Stop!" David yelled.

She kept on swinging the cane at him. "If you think you are going to rob me...you got another thing coming."

"I am not going to rob you," David said as he blocked another blow with his cane. "I'm not a thief. I'm a detective."

The homeless lady stopped as she was about to swing again. "Show me some ID," she said while holding the cane high in the air.

David slowly reached in his back pocket for his billfold. With one hand he held it out to her. She squinted as she read the badge. "Well why didn't you say so? A lady has to be careful nowadays." She smiled a wide smile. Her gold-capped tooth shone even in the dim light. That was the golden glare in his dream.

"What is your name?" he asked.

She stood up tall, as tall as five-foot-nothing would carry her. "My name is Ruby."

David returned her smile. "Well it is nice to meet you, Ruby." He began to pick up her things that fell out of the shopping cart. Her prized possessions were someone else's junk. David knew that this meeting was part of his dream. "Ruby...I wonder if you may help me?"

She gave him a curious look. "Help you how?"

"I am looking for a special necklace."

Ruby's smile returned larger than life. "You have come to the right place," she said as she opened one side of her coat. Hanging down from inside her coat was a cluster of old necklaces. "Take your pick for twenty dollars."

David searched through the assortment of necklaces, some even rusted. The crimson key was not there. "Sorry...not what I'm looking for."

Ruby quickly swung her other arm, opening another array of necklaces. David searched frantically through the mass of chains. The crimson key was still lost. Ruby could see the disappointment on David's face. She then pulled up a sleeve. "How about a bracelet?"

David shook his head. "Sorry...not what I'm looking for." Then he handed her his card. "If you find a necklace, give me a call."

Ruby watched David as he hobbled back towards the alley. "I have a broken one I will let go cheap," she yelled.

David stopped in his tracks. He then turned to face her. She reached into her side pocket and pulled out a necklace, holding it high in the air. David recognized the crimson key dangling on the end of the broken chain. He smiled and began his way back to her.

"The chain is broken...so I will let it go for ten dollars."

David approached her with a smile. "And how much for a chain to replace the broken one?"

Ruby pulled out a silver chain. "You seem like a nice man...it is still twenty dollars."

David reached to his back pocket once again. He opened his wallet and pulled out a crisp new one-hundred-dollar bill. Ruby's eyes widened at the sight of the bill. He then handed it to her.

"I wish I had change for that but I don't," she said while staring at the bill.

David smiled. "You keep the change."

Ruby's mouth dropped open. Then David leaned in and gave her a kiss on the cheek. "Miss Ruby...you are truly an angel."

Chapter 33

David felt whole again. The crimson key was safely around his neck once more. He felt as if he had captured a part of his history, the only personal possession of his mother's. Now that the case was closed and the necklace found, life may proceed, and maybe Amber would stop haunting his dreams. Until this event David had never believed in ghosts. Now that he had firsthand experience with them, only through dreams, his curiosity was piqued. It left him with many questions about life and death, and also life after death. This was not a life-changing event, but it was one he would never forget.

David headed back to his hotel room, but not before stopping for some medication, a bottle of Captain Morgan. The ordeal and activity had left him exhausted. Not to mention that the doctor had given him strict orders to rest and heal. He began thinking to himself. The doctor would definitely not approve of what he had planned this weekend with Sheridan. But he figured he would relax the rest of this day, then all of tomorrow. That should be plenty of rest before meeting up with Sheridan Saturday morning. Anyway, most of his time this weekend with Sheridan was going to be spent in bed. He smiled at his thoughts. That was considered bed rest too, of course.

The first thing David did was take a steaming hot shower, being careful not to get his wound wet. He then fixed himself a Captain and Coke. Just as he took the first long sip, his phone sprang to life. It was Kimberly calling as she was leaving work.

"Well hello there," David answered in a good mood.

"You seem a bit chipper," Kimberly said. "You are either having a Captain or you had a good day."

"Both," he responded. "I found the key."

"That's great! Where did you find it?"

David sat comfortably in a chair, taking his second hit of Captain. "A homeless lady had found it... It was just like in the dream. Amber led me back to the alley. I saw her write something in the snow with her finger. It was a name, Ruby. The name of the homeless lady was Ruby."

"I told you so," Kimberly said excitedly. "She was leading you to the necklace. I can't explain it but it really happened."

"It did. If you had asked me several weeks ago if I believed in ghosts, I would have laughed as I said no."

"What now?" Kimberly asked. "There is nothing keeping you in New York City now."

Thoughts of Sheridan raced through his mind. "Do you remember me telling you about another missing person case I was going to look into for a friend?"

"Yes," she replied. "But I was hoping you were going back later for that. I miss you. And you can't work like you are."

David hesitated, thoughts of the upcoming weekend pictured in his mind. He knew he was going to have to make a decision about Sheridan, even though he and Kimberly had no commitments between them. It still made him feel guilty, and he thought too much of Kimberly to string her along. "Most of this case will be done behind the desk, I promise. If I start on it this weekend, then I should be home by the middle of the week. That way I will not have to return to New York City."

"If you think that's best," Kimberly said, disappointed. "It seems like forever since I've seen you."

"I promise to take care of this business in the next few days," he said, but what he really meant was he promised to make a decision about his future with Sheridan. "When I get back I want you to help me pick out a headstone for Mom's grave. And maybe put something on there about her twin sister Amber."

"That would be sweet…and of course I will help you with anything."

David ended the call and downed his last swallow. He fixed him another Captain while he looked over the hotel menu. He figured he would stay in and relax; that's what room service was for. His phone, still warm from the last call, sprang to life once again. This time it was Sheridan.

"Hello darling," she said in her own sexy voice.

The sound of her voice aroused David instantly. "How did you know I was thinking of you?"

She sighed. "It's that special connection we have. How are you feeling?"

He took a long sip. "Getting better by the minute. Doctor put me on bed rest until Monday."

"That's good," she responded. "That is what I had planned anyway."

David smiled. They talked for another hour. The more they talked, the more his decision swayed in her favor. Thoughts raced through his mind as they talked. They shared a unique bond he had never experienced before, and definitely not the same as with Kimberly. He wasn't sure what it was, maybe because it was new. Whatever it was, it felt wonderful. Either way he knew he had to decide one way or another. David wanted to tell Sheridan his real name and everything about why he came to New York City. He felt it best to wait and tell her everything in person. Then they would also discuss their future, if she felt the same as he did. If so, would they decide to be together in New York City, or would she take this chance to get far away from her father?

Chapter 34

After his conversation with Sheridan, David ordered a rib eye steak. It arrived some time later as David was polishing off his third Captain. While enjoying his meal, thoughts of his conversation with Kimberly popped into his mind. If things did not work out with Sheridan, then he would definitely want to return home as soon as possible. Even if he and Sheridan didn't end up together, he felt obligated to look into her case for her. So to get the ball rolling he decided to begin his investigation. Sheridan did not go into great detail about her mother, but she was suspicious of her father's involvement, which blossomed into great resentment for the man. David decided to begin at this angle and learn what he could of her father, Senator Robert Blakely.

David ate the last morsel of his steak and then took out his laptop. He googled Senator Robert Blakely. The search engine revealed the Senator's own web address.

With a click of his wireless mouse, David found himself face to face with the man. A large picture of him adorned the homepage, smiling from ear to ear with a typical politician's smile. David stared into his eyes as if he were sitting in front of him in real life. He wondered what secrets lay hidden behind that smile and those bright blue eyes. Sheridan shared his eyes.

David searched through the web site. He found nothing of significance, mostly political views and speaking engagements. The Senator had one scheduled in Manhattan this Sunday, which was why Sheridan wanted to get out of the city. He clicked back to the search engine to see what else popped up under the Senator's name. David searched through numerous Facebook and blog comments about the Senator, some in favor of his views and some against.

David's eyes fell to the lower right corner of his screen. The time was 8:13 p.m., past time for his medication. He limped over to the counter top to get it. Picking up the bottle he noticed a warning label: Do Not Take with Alcohol. David shook his head. "Too late for that now," he thought. He popped the pills and washed them down with Captain. He limped over to the nearby window where he looked out over Manhattan. The city lights were magnificent. The sky had cleared and the moon shone bright.

The combination of a full belly, alcohol, and pain medication left David drowsy. He turned and headed to bed, ignoring his laptop, letting it fall to sleep on its own. The screen blackened to sleep just as David cut out the lights. It did not take long for him to drift off to sleep. He slept hard and peaceful for most of the night. Then in the wee hours of the morning he began to dream. Once again he was watching himself as if from afar. He watched himself sleeping serenely as the lights from the city and bright moon above gave dim illumination throughout most of his room.

Movement caught the corner of his eye. It was his mother, Amber in that same red dress. Her long hair flowed behind her as she moved through the room, as if weightless. She stopped at the computer and the screen jumped to life. Amber then went to the closet where David's jacket hung neatly. Her hand went straight to the secret compartment as if she knew something was hidden there. When her hand reappeared, it was holding David's book he kept his notes in, the same one he tore pages out of and gave to Lieutenant Jacoby.

Amber slowly thumbed through the book until she came to the page she searched for. She moved back through the room, her eyes locked on David as she smiled, until she reached the computer once again. She carefully placed the book down, opened at the page she intended. Once again she returned to David's side and sat gently by his side. David watched as she smiled and stroked his hair as he lay sleeping. The crimson key rose out from under his shirt and she caressed it in the palm of her hand. A creaking noise arose, sounding like a rusty hinge to a door. A dim light shone from one side of the room through a door that was not present. Amber looked to the open door with fear in her eyes. A harsh draft filled the room, awakening David from his sleep in his dream.

David's first clear vision was of his mother sitting on the bed next to him, fear consuming her face. The draft began to pull her spirit towards the open door. He instantly reached out for her and her for him. Amber's spirit slipped through his fingertips as she was pulled away. As she disappeared through the door, it quickly shut and vanished. David watched himself rise quickly out of bed and run to where the door once was. All he found was a bare wall, no sign of the door or Amber. David watched himself as he frantically ran his hands across the wall, searching for the door and calling out his mother's name.

David rose quickly in bed, breathing heavily, his hair and face wet with sweat, his pulse racing. He then realized he was dreaming. The bright red numbers on the clock on the nightstand revealed that it was just 4:30 in the morning. A dull pain filled his wounded leg. He rose out of bed and limped to the bathroom by the bright city lights gleaming through the window. He washed his face, then filled a paper cup with cold water. Limping gingerly, he made his way to the counter and spilled out several more pain pills. He slung them into his mouth and forced them down with the cold water. Rest broken, he went back to bed, not realizing the significance of the dream he just had.

Chapter 35

The next time David glanced at the clock it was 7:20 a.m. He awoke tired, but the pain medication he had taken nearly three hours previous was still working. His only pain was in his armpits from the activity the day before with the crutches. Once again he made good use of room service by ordering breakfast. He decided to take a quick shower while he waited for it. As he passed by the computer, he reached over and stabbed the on button with his first finger. It awoke to where he had left it.

The pulsating hot water from the shower massaged David's body and revived his muscles and mind. It lured the memory of his dream from the depths of his consciousness. He stood motionless as if rooted while he replayed the dream in his mind. Curiosity drew him back into the room while still drying. He walked slowly toward the closet as he dried his hair with one towel and used another as a garment. He remembered Amber retrieving his notebook from his jacket, but why, he asked himself, as he slipped it from its hiding place. He thumbed through the book slowly, not knowing what to look for.

David dressed and returned to his work table. When room service knocked, he rose to greet his breakfast. After tipping, he pulled the cart on wheels over by the table. Normally the smell of the bacon would draw his full attention at this point, but thoughts of his dream took priority. He parked the cart to one side so he could eat and satisfy his curiosity at the same time. As he chewed on a crispy piece of bacon, he picked up the notebook and eyed the page it was turned to. The name Angela Graham was at the top with the words Amber's roommate written beneath. Then beneath that he had written "missing three days after she filed a missing person report on Amber Paige."

David's head rose gradually as he thought. Her case was closed as unsolved just like Amber's. His eyes fell back to the page before him. Just beneath was written the name Victoria Cromwell. His eyes widened with surprise as he read the next line: sister of Angela who lives in Albany, New York. His pulse raced with excitement as his eyes turned to the computer screen. "My dream…Amber," he thought. "She is trying to tell me something."

David returned to his breakfast, his eggs cooling down fast. He ate hurriedly as he searched the web for information on a Victoria Cromwell from Albany, New York. The results popped up quickly, her phone number and address on Hillcrest Road. David made a note of them. He searched for a street map of Albany. He soon found that Albany sat on the west bank of the Hudson River, just south of the Mohawk River. Mrs. Victoria Cromwell lived on the northern side of the city, I87 running near her neighborhood, adjacent to the Albany International Airport.

David had all the information he needed and documented in his notebook. He peered at the clock, 8:31 a.m. Still early but most people were up by now, he thought. So he decided to try a call. The phone buzzed on the other end as David waited impatiently. After the fifth ring, the answering machine took charge. David did not really want to leave a message. He would rather talk to a live person instead of a machine. The brief introduction ended, then the all-familiar beep sounded, time for David's part. "Hello Mrs. Cromwell…my name is David Paige. I am calling you concerning Amber Paige and your sister Angela…"

Before David could finish Angela's name, the phone picked up on the other end. "Hello…this is Victoria Cromwell," a sweet voice answered.

"Mrs. Cromwell, I'm sorry to bother you this early but I wish to speak with you at your convenience about Amber Paige."

"What was your name again?" she asked.

"David Paige."

"Are you related to Amber Paige?"

"Yes maam," David replied. "She is my birth mother."

"Oh my," she responded. "I never knew she was pregnant."

"How well did you know Amber?"

She hesitated. "Not very…Angela brought her to my wedding in September of 1986. She was a very beautiful lady."

"Thank you. Did your sister Angela ever speak to you about her?

"Only once," she replied, then paused. "Angela called me for some advice when Amber came up missing. I suggested she file a missing person report." Her voice saddened. "I often wonder if that was the reason for her own disappearance."

Silence filled the phone. "I am sorry if it was," David said. "I see that her case also was never solved."

"My husband was a lawyer and checked into the case at the time. He thought the police department, or the detective handling the case, was covering up something. I guess I will never know what happened to my sister."

David could sense anguish in her voice and wanted to ease some of her pain. "He was right. Our investigation turned up a dirty cop, Pete Sullivan. He was working your sister's case as well as my mother's. Someone was paying him to destroy evidence. That someone was William Nelson. He was responsible for my mother's disappearance and more than likely your sister's after she filed the missing person report." The line went silent. "I thought you would want to know this. Hopefully it will help put your mind at ease."

The line was still silent, but David could hear her breathing. Then he heard a sniffle. "Thank you. It does help to know. You have been a big help, and I appreciate it. You must be a fine young man with traits like your mother. But I still don't understand why Angela never mentioned that Amber had a son."

"She probably didn't know," David responded. "I was born two months after your wedding. I was a preemie. She gave me away to her twin sister, Alice, for my protection just after birth. I never knew about any of this until just recently. I have never even seen a picture of her."

"Oh my goodness," she responded. "I have several pictures of her and Angela. They were in Angela's things that I saved after her disappearance. I will be glad to share them with you. It's the least I can do after the information you just gave me."

"That is very sweet of you," David said, trying to contain his excitement. He checked the time. "How about I treat you to lunch at the restaurant of your choice? I should make it to Albany around one p.m."

"That would be lovely. Lombardo's Restaurant on Madison Avenue is a nice place."

"That sounds great. I will call you again when I'm thirty minutes away."

Chapter 36

David dressed and went to rent a car, an SUV since New York was prone to snow at any time. He felt his new Z28 would be safer parked than on an icy road. The sky had cleared to a brilliant blue, much like the sky back in South Carolina, except it was still twenty degrees with the wind chill a shivering thirteen degrees. Still it was a good clear day for driving. David rented a silver Lincoln Navigator just in case the weather made a quick turn for the worse. Once out of Manhattan, the traffic lightened gradually the farther he went. He managed to slip onto I87 and off he flew.

Memories of the dream occupied his mind, overpowering the radio and road noise. He played the dream over and over in his mind as if it were prerecorded somehow. He wondered why this meeting was significant enough to haunt his dreams. No, he did not have a picture of his mother Amber, but through his dreams she had managed to permanently imprint a vision of her in his mind for all time. Maybe like the crimson key, she felt the need for him to have something of hers that he could touch or feel, and with a picture, something to frame for future generations. If this was so important to her, then it was the least he could do. Maybe this would finally put her soul to rest.

David's thoughts shifted to his other mother Alice. Christmas was just a little over three weeks away, his first without her. He remembered how she always loved this time of year, and always did whatever she could to make it special for him too, even after he had outgrown Santa Claus. He missed her dearly, and wondered why she hadn't visited his dreams. Was it she felt bad for keeping Amber and the money a secret until now? He hoped not, because she was only following her heart. There is no way he could be angry at her for that. Plus she filled in as a better mother than he could have possibly dreamed. It would be nice if she would sneak in a dream just to say hi.

David shook his head. "What the hell am I thinking about," he said out loud to himself. He looked up in the mirror at his own reflection. "Now I'm talking to myself." David shook the thoughts out of his head as he read a road sign displaying thirty miles to Albany. His stomach roared as he called Victoria Cromwell. It was so loud that he was afraid she might hear it. He told her his location, and she reminded him of the name and location of the restaurant.

Lombardo's Grill was lit up in neon on a vertical sign mounted to the front of a two-tone rustic building, its style reminiscent of an era pre-1950. David parked the Navigator and stepped out into even more frigid air than when he left Manhattan. His leg was stiff and sore from the three-hour drive. He was well overdue for a pain pill, but he had passed on taking one earlier because it might affect his driving. He slowly limped to the front entrance.

A young clean-cut waiter dressed like a penguin greeted him at the door. David gave him his name. The waiter told him that a table was ready and Mrs. Cromwell was waiting. David explored the restaurant with his eyes as he followed the waiter. A long bar with a beautiful wood grain top stretched outward through one side of the room. A large clear mirror was its backstop. Ceiling fans twirled slowly above. Portions for dining were encased with iconic art murals. Chandeliers hung elegantly from high ceilings, while other areas were set up more casual with old-fashioned booths. Inside and out, Lombardo's had an old world charm about it.

The waiter delivered David to a quaint table for two in a far corner. A beautiful silver-haired thin lady stood with a hand out at his approach. "You must be David," she said as they shook gently.

"And you must be Mrs. Cromwell."

She sat softly. "Please…call me Victoria."

"As you wish, Victoria," David said as he looked around. "You have great taste in restaurants."

"It is one of the finest in the state of New York. But the prices are much more reasonable than you are used to in Manhattan."

"I am sure that is true," he responded. "But I am not from Manhattan."

"Excuse me…I just assumed."

"That's understandable," he remarked. "I'm from Mount Pleasant, a suburb of Charleston, South Carolina."

"That is a beautiful part of the country. My husband and I spent several weekends there through the years. That also explains your Southern drawl."

The waiter returned for drink and appetizer orders. David had a taste for a Captain and Coke but settled for sweet tea. She preferred water, and both passed on an appetizer. The waiter left for the drinks as David thumbed through the menu. "Italian American cuisine very reasonably priced for the décor and service," he thought to himself.

"May I make a suggestion?" she asked.

"Of course…please do."

"The special of the day is always a right choice," she whispered over her menu. "Everyone thinks because it's cheaper that it's not prepared up to standards. That is quite the opposite. They work harder at preparing it just perfectly because most people order it just to save money. The exquisite taste will keep them coming back time after time."

"That makes good business sense," David remarked. "Thanks for the tip."

"You're welcome," she responded. "I need to go to the ladies room. If the waiter returns while I'm gone, please order me the special of the day."

"Certainly…that will be two specials of the day please."

She smiled a perfect smile to him as she rose and then walked away. David took notice of a manila envelope she had propped against the leg of her chair. He could not keep his eyes off the envelope, imagining what was inside.

Chapter 37

The waiter returned as David was lost in thought staring at the envelope. He cleared his throat intentionally, startling David out of his trance. David ordered two specials of the day as he had told Victoria he would. His eyes and thoughts fell back upon the envelope after the waiter had left. Victoria was making her way back to the table when she noticed David staring at the envelope. She sat back down, breaking his stare. David looked across into her vivid green eyes as she gave him the same smile she had earlier. "Curiosity killed the cat," she said as she reached down for the envelope.

He returned her smile. "I'm sorry. But it is more like anticipation."

She held the envelope in her lap. "If you don't mind, I would love to hear the whole story."

"Certainly," David said, and then began to tell her the story as he knew it. He told about Amber and Alice being twins raised by their grandparents because their mother died giving birth. Then about how Amber went off to New York City in pursuit of a modeling career. He told about the night Amber gave him away to Alice—how she feared for his safety—and about the money as well. He told how Alice took him and moved to Mount Pleasant where he lived his life not knowing of his true beginning. David described his life growing up and then college. He then told her about Alice's death and how he came to learn the truth. Finally he told her everything that had happened to him while in New York City—except for Sheridan and his supernatural dreams, which led him to her.

"This story has the makings of a great book," she said as the food arrived. "And a great movie as well." She returned the envelope to the side of her chair. "Let's enjoy our food, and then we will enjoy the pictures."

David nodded in agreement, though he'd rather go straight to the photographs. They both enjoyed their meal over small talk. Victoria most definitely knew what she was talking about. The lasagna was the best David had ever eaten. They both passed on dessert and ordered coffee instead. The waiter cleared the table before them, space needed for the pictures. David watched as Victoria reached for the envelope again, hoping this time there would be no distractions. He was filled with anticipation. She opened the envelope slowly and poured its contents onto the table in front of her. About a dozen pictures flowed out, many old and slightly discolored from time. They were all taken with an instant camera, which was popular in the eighties.

The picture on top, taken at Victoria's wedding, showed Amber and Angela during the reception. She held each picture for David to see as she explained what was happening at that moment. David marveled at the snapshots. Though some were partially faded, he didn't realize quite how beautiful Amber really was, and how much she resembled herself in his dreams. Her spirit in his dreams didn't seem lifelike, maybe because she wasn't living. The faded pictures brought her to life, even more vivid than he imagined. David was glad he came now. Having a picture, or several if Victoria was willing, would make Amber seem more real to him.

Victoria continued explaining every picture she displayed to David. Unfortunately the pile was dwindling down, with only three left on the table. He was really enjoying the show and wished there were more pictures to go through. She had shown him various poses of Amber, most with her best friend Angela, but some of Amber alone. Victoria picked up the next to the last picture and explained it to David. It was of Amber alone walking down the runway at a show. People lined both sides of the runway like fans at a concert. David took notice of a somewhat familiar face just as Victoria went to the last photo.

David picked up the photo and stared at the face. It seemed familiar, but he couldn't quite place it. "Who is that?" he asked, pointing to the face.

Victoria drew closer, squinting to get a clear view. "I believe," she said, then took the picture from him, holding it even closer to her face. "Yes it is…that is the President."

"The President?" he asked as he took another look at the photo. David glared at the face. "Isn't it strange for him to be there?"

Victoria pointed at the man beside the President. "Not at all. See…there is Senator McKenzie, God rest his soul. Politicians flocked to events like these. Exposure reaps votes."

"Oh," David responded as he lowered the photo onto the pile, thinking nothing else of it.

When he raised his eyes to meet hers, Victoria was wearing a wide smile, holding a picture up facing herself. "Now this is my favorite one. So if you want this picture I would like a copy please." She slowly turned the picture around for David to see. It was the clearest picture in the bunch, preserved as if it had been in a frame for years. It was a picture of Amber and Angela clowning around. They both had their faces pressed together apparently laughing uncontrollably. Amber had held out the camera with one hand and snapped a self-portrait of the two best friends in their apartment. David's smile matched Victoria's. This precious snapshot was definitely a keeper. He could see why she requested a copy.

Victoria watched the expression on David's face change from one of joy to one of shock. "What is it?"

David did not answer at first, only pointed at the picture. "What is that?"

She quickly turned the picture around. "What are you asking about?"

His finger came to rest on the object in question. Behind Amber against the wall, partially hidden by her image, was a wooden object. "Oh that—it's an old wooden trunk." She could see the seriousness in his eyes. "What about it?"

David took the picture from Victoria and held it carefully as if it was a treasure, his eyes glued to it. "That is my mother's trunk. If only I could find it. She had said in a letter that the answer to her demise lay hidden in this trunk…If only I could find it."

Victoria placed a comforting hand on his. "I have that trunk stored in my attic."

Chapter 38

David's eyes rose to meet Victoria's. "You have this trunk?"

"Yes," she replied. "After Angela's disappearance, my husband and I made the trip to Manhattan. We stored everything in the attic. Some of it we weren't sure belonged to Angela or Amber."

"You have this trunk?" he repeated, his face apparently in shock.

She laughed. "Yes, yes, yes," she repeated. "It is in the attic. I didn't know which it belonged to. I'm not sure what good it is to you. We never located the key."

David's look of shock transformed to a wide smile. Victoria watched as his hand dived beneath his shirt at his front collar and, to her own surprise, pulled out a silver chain with a crimson-colored key dangling on the end. She leaned in to get a closer look. "That looks like it may fit."

"Oh it fits for sure," he said. "She wouldn't have led me here if it didn't."

Victoria gave David a confused look. "Who led you here?"

Their eyes met—he wasn't sure whether to mention the dreams or not. "I don't want you to think I'm crazy."

"Unless you are talking about aliens, I won't think you are crazy. I'm probably the crazy one. My dead husband visits me in my dreams."

David laughed.

"I'm serious," she said.

"I'm not laughing at you," he reassured her. "I'm laughing because my mother, Amber has been visiting me in my dreams. She led me to you...to this trunk."

She gave him a weird look. "And I thought I was crazy."

They both laughed out loud.

David picked up the tab as he had promised. He followed close behind Victoria in her white Escalade. She led him to the Latham area near the airport. He remembered the route from his MapQuest search as they turned onto Hillcrest Road. They came to a stop in front of a house that looked similar to the one haunted in Amityville. The two windows at the end of the house peered at him as if the house had eyes. David stepped carefully out of the Navigator, his eyes glued to the house. Victoria smiled as she noticed his stare. "It's not the same house."

"How did you know what I was thinking?" David asked.

"I've seen that look many times before," she replied. "It may be haunted…but my husband is a good ghost."

They both snickered as she unlocked the front door. Once inside, David's eyes fell upon the banister railing, reminiscent of the one in the movie. "Are you sure this is not the same house?"

"Not the same house…but evidently the same architect." She led him to the living room. "Would you like some coffee or tea?"

"Coffee would be nice if it's no trouble."

She smiled. "No trouble at all. I usually keep a pot going. Make yourself at home while I start a pot. Then I will take you to the attic."

David came to rest on a dark leather sofa. The room was spotless with everything in it from the furniture to the pictures on the wall placed meticulously. David noticed there weren't any pictures of children anywhere. After a few minutes Victoria entered carrying two cups of coffee. "If you are ready we will head to the attic."

"May I ask you a personal question?" David asked.

"Why of course you can."

"Do you have children?"

She glanced at him as they walked. "No." She paused. "We weren't able to have children. You must have noticed there weren't any pictures of children in the living room."

"Yes."

"You are very observant. You must be a good detective." She paused. "Angela and I were the only children in my family. So with her disappearance and my not having any children, my wall is free of tiny smiling faces."

"I'm sorry. I shouldn't have asked."

"Nonsense," she responded. "I taught grade school for thirty years. I have had hundreds of children through the years. I just didn't have to clean up after them when I got home." She laughed. "I guarantee if we went to Wal-Mart or the grocery store right now we would run into at least a dozen or more grownups that I once taught. And I guarantee after looking into their eyes I could tell you each of their names along with most of their parents' names."

"You must have loved your job."

"With a passion," she quickly responded. "But after thirty years, I was ready to retire." She unlocked a door on the third floor. "Here we are. You will have to forgive the mess. I haven't been up here for years. There may be a ghost up here for real."

The room was organized much better than she let on. Most of the items were draped with old white sheets, which made it look like a ghost convention in progress. Cobwebs occupied the corners of the room. Dust particles in the air were visible through the evening sun beaming through the windows. The air was chilled but still above freezing.

"Over here," Victoria said as she pulled back a dusty sheet. She uncovered an old love seat and matching chair. "These were in the small apartment."

David caught a glimpse of something wooden behind the chair. He carefully moved the chair out, revealing the wooden antique trunk. His heart raced, pounding within his chest just beneath the crimson key.

"There it is," Victoria said. "Let's take it to a room with heat in it."

"It may be too heavy for us to move with my leg the way it is."

"My husband and I carried it up here," she responded. "Whatever is on the inside must not be very heavy."

Victoria took a sheet and wiped the dust from the trunk. They both grasped a leather handle on opposite ends and lifted it gingerly. Like she had said, it was lighter than he expected. Whatever mystery was hidden within didn't carry very much weight.

Chapter 39

Victoria and David carried the trunk to the first warm room they approached, a spare bedroom twice the average size. They set the trunk down in the middle of the room. David reached behind his neck and unclasped the silver chain. He took the key in hand and lowered it to the keyhole. The trunk was rectangular-shaped with black hinges and corner braces. The latch with the keyhole exposed was also black. David wondered why the key was painted crimson red with fingernail polish. Maybe it was just Amber's favorite color since in his dreams she was always wearing the same red dress.

The key slipped into the keyhole perfectly. A gentle twist and the latch popped open. David looked up at Victoria; a wide smile covered her face. He slowly lifted the top until it leaned slightly back, keeping the trunk open. The inside was entirely covered in crimson red velvet. The inside of the top was bordered in thick white lace. In the center near the top was a portrait of Amber glued to the velvet. The portrait looked like a glamour shot of her in a red low-cut evening dress, like the one in David's dreams. David could not remove his eyes from the portrait. She was the most beautiful woman he had ever seen. His eyes finally dropped to the bottom. All he found were three old photo albums. Victoria watched as he opened the oldest-looking one. It contained pictures, apparently, of Amber's grandparents who raised her, along with a picture of a pretty young teenager. The resemblance made David think she was Amber and Alice's mother, his grandmother.

Victoria put a comforting hand on David's shoulder. "You are seeing your family history for the first time. I will leave you alone with your thoughts. Take whatever time you need. I will be downstairs if you need anything."

David rendered her a smile of thanks and returned to his heritage. Hours passed as he slowly looked over each and every photo, examining everyone very closely, though they all looked were strangers to his eyes. He wondered what kind of personalities they possessed, their likes and dislikes. So much of his ancestry had been kept a secret from him, all because of his evil father. His thoughts returned to the night in the alley when his father had stabbed him. Would his father have embraced him had he known his son stood before him? Or would he have just blown his brains out as he did the cab driver? David angered at his thoughts.

Victoria entered the room. "You must be hungry by now. How about a dinner break?"

David looked up into her eyes. "You have a restaurant in mind?"

"As a matter of fact I do," she replied. "Mine— dinner is ready. All you have to do is wash up."

"You shouldn't have gone to so much trouble."

She smiled. "Actually it was a pleasure. It's not often I get a chance to cook for someone."

David washed up and joined her in the dining room. He sat down to a wonderful meal of fried chicken, string beans, mashed potatoes, homemade biscuits, and gravy. "Now I am getting homesick."

"I'm glad you approve."

David tasted the gravy. "Are you sure you aren't from the South?"

She laughed. "New Yorker all my life. But my granny lived in Virginia. I spent several summers with her. She taught me how to cook."

"And a fine job she did," he remarked as he took a bite of fried chicken. "I haven't had a meal like this since…" He stopped.

"After today and what you told me of your life, you have been through a lot lately."

He wiped his mouth. "My life—or what I thought was my life—has been turned upside down in the past several weeks."

"I could see it in your eyes upstairs. You were looking at pictures of complete strangers, yet they were your family. That's got to be hard."

"What makes it so hard is that there is no one else left in my family. I don't have a brother, sister, cousin, or any kind of relative that I can talk to. Someone to tell me stories about my grandfather or grandmother. Especially funny stories of things they did in their lives when growing up. All I have is pictures with no memories."

"I have a suggestion, not a cure," she said, catching his attention. "Start your own string of memories. Memories that your children and their children will always remember, talk about, and laugh together as they recollect. Don't let this family end with you...let it begin."

David suddenly thought of Sheridan and Kimberly, a decision to be made.

"May I ask you a personal question?" Victoria asked.

"But of course."

"What now?" she asked sincerely.

David thought hard. "I should head back to South Carolina. That is where my heart is and my future lies. I haven't been able to admit it before now...at least not until you just opened my eyes." He sat back in his chair. "Thank you for that fine meal...and eye-opening advise."

"Not so fast," she said. "You haven't had dessert. How about old-fashioned chocolate chess pie? It is my grandmother's recipe."

David smiled at the sound of chocolate chess. "Can I adopt you for a mother? You would be my number three."

They both laughed out loud.

Chapter 40

David enjoyed the chocolate chess pie and asked for the recipe. Kimberly loved to cook and this would make a great addition to her offerings. Evening turned into night and 9 p.m. approached. Victoria invited David to spend the night. He could sack out in the room with the trunk. He graciously accepted her invitation. It would be for the better this way, he thought, away from New York City, away from Sheridan. He decided to call her in the morning and break it off with her. He had made his decision—his heart belonged to Kimberly. Sheridan and he had a special connection, one he had never experienced before, and it remained a mystery to him. He knew if he followed through with their plans in the mountains that this special connection would draw him into her arms regardless of how he felt for Kimberly and regardless of the decision he had made. No, that connection with Sheridan could no longer stand between himself and his roots, his deep and mature love for Kimberly. David was in agreement with himself—call Sheridan in the morning.

David retired to his room. He stopped at the trunk, staring down at the three photo albums inside. His eyes then rose to the glamour shot glued to the top, drowned in a red velvet background, complimenting the red dress she was wearing. She was a true beauty for the ages, his mother. He swept up the three photo albums from inside and laid them out on the bed. He began thumbing through the one with the pictures of Amber and Alice's childhood. Thoughts of Kimberly filled his mind, wishing she was here sharing this moment with him. So he decided to do the next best thing, call her.

Kimberly and David talked for over an hour. He told her about the latest dream and how he found the trunk. Then he went on and on about the pictures inside, the family he never knew. He also talked about Victoria, Amber's roommate's sister, and how kind she had been. He wanted Kimberly to meet her someday. David and Kimberly both grew tired but didn't want to hang up. Finally, while nodding, David ended the call with an I love you forever. Kimberly was too tired and sleepy to grasp the significance of what he had just said.

In his exhaustion, David fell into a deep sleep on top of the comforter, fully clothed with his cell still in hand. Amber came to him once again in a dream. He could clearly see her and himself hugging, as if she was finally happy that he had found the trunk with the family pictures inside. Strangely, though, they were not in this room next to the trunk but standing on the white fur rug at the house in the mountains. He could not understand why, unless it was simply because she first entered his dreams there.

David's heart swelled as he watched, the mother he never knew. His eyes watered, and tears gently ran down each side of his cheeks, as if competing to see which one reached the bottom first. Then Amber jerked her head in the direction of the door to the wine cellar. The door slowly screeched open halfway, as if riding on dull rusty hinges. She quickly turned her head back to David with fear-stricken eyes, hugging him tighter, as if hanging on for dear life. The draft began lifting all the lightweight items in the room. They spun around in midair, much as they did in the Poltergeist movie. Then Amber's spirit began to stretch, pulled helplessly to the cracked door. Tears rushed down her cheeks. David clawed at her image, but his fingers passed right through her transparent body. Helplessly he watched her as she was sucked away. In an effort to save her, he ran to the door. Jerking it wide open, he stared into the stairway.

David watched himself as fear flushed his face. His eyes opened wide as he leaned back, frightened to death of what stood before him. Suddenly, three bony arms and hands reached through the doorway. They each grabbed hold of David by his shirt. They yanked him through the doorway and the door slammed shut behind him.

David leaped up in bed, eyes darting in the darkness as if still engulfed in the nightmare. He was sweating profusely and breathing heavily, his pulse racing. A sudden beating on the door made him jump. "David!" Victoria yelled in panic. "Are you all right?"

David limped to the door and opened it. "Yes, I think so…it was just a dream."

"I believe it must have been a nightmare. I heard you yell out as if a monster had a hold of you."

David wiped his forehead with the sleeve of his shirt. "I think it did."

"Was it your mother again?"

He wiped his face as he sat on the edge of the bed. "Yes…but I don't understand. She has been haunting my dreams, but nothing as bad as this one. She helped me find the lost key, and I did. She led me to you, to the trunk, and I found it. I have the photo albums of the family I never knew that she left for me. The mission is complete. So why is she still haunting me? Am I missing something here?"

They both walked over to the trunk. David remembered something Mick from the locksmith shop had told him, that they sometimes had secret compartments. He felt around on the inside. It was solid all around the edges with no apparent secret hiding place. He straightened up and ran his fingers through his hair. "There is nothing else there."

"Are you planning to take the trunk with you when you leave?"

He shook his head. "I was hoping you would keep it for a while. I have a Z28 in storage back in New York City. There is no way it would fit. I would like to come back one day in a truck or SUV. There is a special lady in my life I would like you to meet. I also would like to keep in touch. You are the closest thing I have to family now. You are the only living person I know who actually knew my mother when she was alive."

"That sounds great. But you will have to stay with me a whole weekend. I could show this special lady of yours some of my grandmother's recipes."

"That is right down her alley," he responded. "She loves to cook."

Chapter 41

David hopped in the shower to wash off his sweat. Hot pulsating water relaxed his stiffened muscles. The nightmare lingered in his mind. Confused at the meaning, he tried to dismiss it from his thoughts. He returned to the bed, glancing at the clock on the wall, 2:13 a.m. This time he crawled between the sheets instead of crashing on top. He tossed and turned, unable to sleep or frightened of reliving the nightmare. With a narrow eye, he checked the time once again, 2:33 a.m. Only twenty minutes had elapsed.

Tired but unable to sleep, he rose and limped to the window. He peered out into the moon-drenched yard. The moon was dazzling, illuminating everything but the shadows it forced from the trees. The snow on the ground glowed, like neon lighting. His leg began to ache. He decided to take a pain pill, hoping it would help him get some sleep. While he was flushing the pill down with water, David stared at the open trunk.

His mother's picture glued to the red felt top stared back. He rose and walked slowly to the trunk, drawn by her photo. The trunk was still empty and still haunting him. He reached for the top to close it once and for all, hoping the nightmare would be trapped inside forever. A thought crossed his mind. He had to have this picture for his collection. It was the best one of all, expressing her natural beauty.

David dropped slowly to one knee, examining the edge of the photo. With a careful finger, he gently began peeling from a loose corner. The picture peeled off easier than he thought it would, intact and still perfect. He held the picture close, admiring his beautiful mother as he rose to his feet. He opened one of the albums to where he remembered seeing a vacant slot. The picture fit perfectly, as if it had been there at one time. David closed the album carefully and stacked the three in a chair next to his shirt so he wouldn't forget to take them. He was eager to share them with Kimberly.

David's eyes grew heavy from the medication kicking in. As he reached to cut off the lamp by the bed, his eyes drifted back to the trunk and he realized he had never shut the top. He peeled the covers back and rose out of bed. As he limped towards the trunk, his eyes narrowed. Where the picture had been glued was a hole in the red velvet. He dropped to one knee to get a better view. It was definitely a hole, a deep one at that, too dark to see inside the cavity. David rose and went to retrieve his trusty penlight. On his return, he cast a beam of light into the hole. Deep inside was another keyhole, painted in crimson red fingernail polish.

David's eyes widened in surprise—a secret compartment as Mick had said. He carefully placed the crimson key in the hole. The depth equaled the length of the key. He turned the key with anticipation. The whole panel of red velvet fell into his hands. The edges had been cleverly hidden by the thick lace that surrounded the inside of the top, disguised and not noticeable to the naked eye. The keyhole also had been cleverly hidden behind Amber's photo, a photo she knew he would not leave behind. Once he took the picture, he would find the secret keyhole that the crimson key would unlock, the secret to her demise.

Behind the hidden panel was a brown document-size envelope. David lifted it out and peeked inside. More photos of some kind occupied the envelope. He walked back to the bed and poured out the contents. Pictures spilled out onto wrinkled covers, about a dozen in all. David sat on the edge of the bed and laid the envelope down on the comforter. He picked up the closest picture, drawing it closer to his face. It was just a picture of the inside of a house. Though it was taken twenty-five years ago, it looked familiar to David. He stared relentlessly at it. Then his eyes widened as he figured out where this photo was taken—inside the house in the mountains that belonged to Sheridan's father, Senator Robert Blakely. The furniture and décor were somewhat different, but the distinctive fireplace and layout were unmistakable. This confused him, and he grabbed another picture. Sure enough, that was the place. This picture was taken from outside, showing the house from the driveway. The view of the mountains in the background was a dead giveaway. That was one of the first things David had admired.

David took up another photo. It was taken from inside the house but through the window. Blakely was in the yard, evidently unaware he was being photographed. David looked through more photos of the house, inside and out. She was there, he thought, not grasping the reality of the situation. He then picked up the last one, a very damaging photo. It was a picture of Blakely sleeping in his bed. The covers were entangled, as if he had struggled with someone before passing out. Then to one side of the photo was a reflection in the full-length mirror from the opened closet door. The reflection was of Amber standing in the nude on the other side of the room. She had a camera raised to her eye, taking this very picture.

David fell back on the bed. "This can't be," he thought to himself. "So this is what she wanted me to find." He rose back up, shaking his head. "Senator Robert Blakely is my father. The evil bastard who wanted my life aborted." Hatred filled his soul. Then another shocking revelation struck him—Sheridan was his half-sister. Now he understood the special connection he felt toward her. It was in the blood, not in the hormones. His eyes widened as he thought of the weekend they spent together. "I made love to my sister," he thought, then rose and paced the floor. Now his plans had changed. Sheridan needed to see these pictures for herself. Instead of a dear Jane call, it would be proper to meet with her and explain the whole awkward situation to her. David flopped back down on the pillow, thoughts racing through his mind. But the medication was pulling at his eyelids again. He drifted off to sleep once again on top of the covers, pictures strewn across crumpled sheets.

Chapter 42

David woke to the aroma of fresh-cooked bacon. He rolled over glancing at the clock, 6:13 a.m. He rolled back over, not wanting to get up, but he knew Victoria would be expecting him. So out of courtesy to her, he forced himself up. After washing up he headed to the kitchen, leaving the pictures on the bed the way they were. Thoughts of his discovery haunted his mind as he jolted a burst of caffeine into his tired body. The coffee tasted as good as it did back home. He savored the coffee and breakfast equally. They both enjoyed small talk as they ate. David did not tell her of his unearthing last night, that his real father was Senator Robert Blakely. This discovery carried many implications about Amber's demise for sure and quite possibly Angela's as well. He decided it best to wait until he had hard evidence to support the theory. With this discovery, the police would most definitely reopen both cases, prying deep into the Senator's affairs. But first he wanted to tell Sheridan himself, alone. This bombshell would definitely cause a media frenzy. He wanted Sheridan spared from as much of it as possible.

After a long delicious breakfast, David returned to his room. He placed the panel back in place inside the trunk, locking it securely with the crimson key. He then lowered the top, locking it as well. He placed the trunk against the wall out of the way for safe keeping. David approached the bed, staring down at the pictures, thoughts and feelings raging throughout his body. He picked up the envelope to place the pictures back inside when he felt a lump, something he had missed. Peeking inside, he saw a folded paper. He reached in and sprung the paper loose. It was a letter to him from Amber, written on plain notebook paper. David began to read it. It told of the whole affair she had with Senator Robert Blakely, and how he was the only man she had been with for the past two years. She went on to tell him that Blakely was his father, and that he threatened her if she did not have an abortion, but that he was really in love with her.

David snarled as he read, his anger reaching the boiling point. "You thought I was a threat to your career back then," he thought to himself. "Just wait until this gets out."

She explained how the threat opened her eyes, and that she had decided not to go through with it, even if it meant her life. She told him of her plans to move away temporarily until after he was born. Then she planned on letting Alice raise him out of harm's way. She reassured him in the letter that Blakely did not even know she had a sister. She was certain he would be safe with her. She wanted him to know that if anything ever happened to her that Blakely would be the one responsible. Amber went into detail about how Blakely wanted a divorce from his wife, but she was pregnant and it would be devastating to his career. He had joked about her being in an accident and her body never found. Amber wasn't sure if he was joking or serious, even though he had laughed at the thought. The letter revealed that she was frightened of him, but trapped. The letter ended with I Love You Forever.

David's rage was apparent by the way he stuffed the letter back into the envelope. He picked up the pictures, straightening them like a deck of cards. His phone sprang to life on the nightstand, jittering like a june bug flipped on its back. His eyes swung to the clock, 7 a.m. "Sheridan," he murmured under his breath. "Curtain time."

"Hello darling," Sheridan answered in a cheery mood. "Are you ready for me to play doctor?"

"Hello Sheridan."

"Okay, what's wrong? You haven't called me Sheridan since we consummated our relationship."

"I'm sorry...my leg is killing me this morning," he lied.

"I'm sorry, baby. I promise to make you feel better. I will pick you up at eight sharp."

"There has been a change in plans."

"What?" she remarked.

"I'm not in the hotel. I have run across some information about your father that I need to show you."

"You have already begun on my case. No wonder your leg hurts."

"Yes I have," he lied again. "I'm in Albany."

"What are you doing in Albany? Does this mean our get-together is canceled?"

"I found a source in Albany that has enlightened me. Our get-together is still on. I will drive down and meet you there instead."

"That is great. I was afraid you had changed your mind about us."

"No," he lied again. "It is urgent that I see you."

"I like the way you said that," she responded. "I will see you at noon with bells on, and probably nothing else."

"Looking forward to it." Another lie, and becoming too easy. David ended the call with a smooching noise, then grimaced at the thought of Sheridan being his half-sister.

Chapter 43

David regretted the lies, but regretted even more this reunion with Sheridan. How she was going to react was his biggest worry. Was she going to get angry and throw him out before he could explain everything to her? He rehearsed their conversation as he drove, talking out loud and gesturing with his hand as if she were right there in front of him. Cars passed slowly, the occupants staring strangely at David as they went by, believing him looney. David just smiled and waved just before they floored it. Over and over he tried to figure out the best way to tell her. He even played in his mind what to say if she lost it and threw a hissy fit.

David pulled through the front gate, confident he had the situation under control. As he parked next to his father's Hummer, thoughts of what Sheridan had said flashed into his mind—she would be waiting with bells on and probably nothing else. David swallowed hard at the thought. Expecting to be flashed or mooned by her, he slowly opened the door. What came rushing out caught him by surprise. It was not Sheridan in her birthday suit but instead the wonderful aroma of fresh-cooked bacon. "Coming in!" he called out.

Sheridan returned his call, "In the kitchen!"

Relieved to see her fully clothed, he approached her reluctantly, envelope in hand. She turned to face him and their eyes locked instantly. All that time and effort David spent rehearsing and embarrassing himself on the interstate was a waste. He suddenly found himself speechless as he stared into her eyes, his mind blank. "Where is my hello kiss?" she asked with hands on her hips.

"Right here," David replied as he went to her quickly.

Sheridan greeted him with open arms and the intent to take his breath away with a seductive kiss. David bounced his lips off hers and fell into a big hug. Shock and confusion filled her face as she rested her head on his left shoulder. "That felt more like a kiss from a relative," she said as she pulled back and looked into his eyes. "Is there something wrong? Something you are not telling me?"

David took her by a hand, leading her to the table. "There is so much I need to tell you about your father." He released her hand and took a seat, resting the envelope in the center of the table.

"The bacon is ready. All we have to do is put the sandwiches together. Can't this wait a bit?"

David looked deep into her eyes. "No…this is too important to sit on."

Sheridan sat down slowly. "You are scaring me, David. Have you found out something about my mother?"

"No…not really," he answered. "I haven't had a chance to check into your mother. But I have found out a lot about your father. And you are not going to like what I found."

Sheridan's expression turned to anger. "You have probably found out something that I have been suspecting all along."

David picked up the envelope. "Probably…and a lot more." He paused. "There is something I need to tell you now."

His conversation was abruptly ended by a loud screeching sound, like a door on extremely rusted hinges. Both of their heads turned towards the eerie sound. The door to the cellar had opened about halfway. David leaped to his feet. "Just like in my dream," he spit out quickly.

Sheridan stared at him with a raised brow. "Dream? That door has come open like that before. It definitely needs oiling."

David's head snapped back towards her. "You heard that sound…the screeching?"

"Yes of course," she replied, staring harder at him. "It just needs a little oil."

David's eyes returned to the door. "No…when I checked that door last weekend it glided easily and did not make a sound."

Sheridan shook her head. "So…maybe it needs a little now."

David shook his head continuously, reliving his nightmare in his mind. "No...this is just the way it sounded in my dream." He inched slowly towards the door.

Sheridan rose to her feet. "David...what dream? And what were you about to tell me? What has this to do with my father?"

David stopped, realizing he still had the envelope in his hand. His eyes darted back, meeting hers. "I have to check this out. You wouldn't understand...trust me." He stepped back, handing her the envelope. "It's all in here. I will be right back to explain everything."

Sheridan took the envelope as a confused expression filled her face. She could not understand why David was acting so strangely. She shook her head at him, then began to open the envelope. David inched quietly and carefully to the door, as if sneaking up on someone. He placed a hand on the door and jerked it open quickly. A sigh of relief leaped from his mouth. He moved the door back and forth. It glided as if on silk hinges—not a sound did it make. David stared into the darkness of the stairway before him. He rose on his toes while stretching his neck like a turtle to get a better look.

Confident that a monster with bony hands, like the one in his dream, was not about to attack him and jerk him down the steps, he reached in and switched on the light. The bulb blinked to life, revealing nothing before him but empty steps.

"That bastard," Sheridan said loudly with anger in his voice.

David knew Sheridan was reading the letter, but didn't dare turn his head back in her direction, from fear that once he looked back he would be attacked by the bony monster in his dream.

Chapter 44

David carefully made his way down the steps. He could hear Sheridan behind him upstairs, cursing under her breath. He could only imagine what her reaction was going to be after he revealed his true identity. The thought distracted him momentarily while he stood in the faint lighting at the foot on the steps. He reached out and pulled down on the old chain before him. The light bulb blinked several times before coming to life. David's eyes slowly swept the cellar from his left to his right. Sweat dripped from his nervous brow. His thoughts returned to his dream and what it could have meant. There was nothing down here unexplainable. The only thing he could not explain, and it seemed somewhat petty, was the creaking door.

"David!" Sheridan called out.

"Coming," he called back as he reached for the chain. Then suddenly the strange feeling he had had once before returned, but much stronger this time, as if something was physically pulling him towards where the wine cellar narrowed. This time David followed his feeling rather than his eyes, letting himself be drawn into the cavern-shaped room. He moved slowly, heart racing, watching for the bony monster in his dream. Cold sweat filled his forehead, inching down the sides of his face. He stopped, as a deathly cold chill passed through his body. His eyes were strangely drawn to the wine rack before him. There before him stood a single bottle of wine to itself—not a bottle within five feet on either side, nor any above or below. He looked around at the colossal wine rack. Every slot but a few was occupied. He wondered why this one bottle sat to itself, and strangely at the exact spot where he was drawn to. He grasped the neck of the cool dusty bottle and pulled it out carefully. With his free hand he wiped the dust from the label. But rather than dropping to the ground, the dust swirled and drew back into the rack, mysteriously sucked towards the wall behind.

David dropped a hand to where the dust swirled. A slight draft danced across his fingers. He took his trusty penlight from his pocket and bent over for a better view. With a narrow beam of light he stabbed the empty slot where the bottle had sat. Behind the wine rack was a wall of wide oak boards. David's eyes fell upon movement. Between two boards that weren't sealed together was a noticeable gap. There in the middle of the gap was a large dust bunny dancing about from a draft.

David straightened up and took a step backwards. He took notice of how this part of the wall protruded out from the rest. He tried to picture in his mind the shape of the house at the rear. To his recollection it was straight across. As he wondered, he noticed the label on the bottle of wine still clutched in his hand. It said 1986 Caymus Cabernet Franc. Just below was written in bold letters: Amber Wine.

David's eyes and mouth flew open, his heart jumped. "She is here," he thought. He set the bottle to the side, out of the way, and began emptying the rack. Bottles clinked together as he worked hurriedly, as if attempting to save a dying person.

"David!" Sheridan yelled from the doorway up the steps. "What are you doing down there?"

David wiped his sweaty brow. "I need some help."

Sheridan made her way to the cellar, still clutching the letter. She approached him with a confused look. "What the hell are you doing?"

David knew the anger in her voice was from the letter and not aimed at him, at least not yet. "Think," he said. "The back side of the house—is it straight across or does it dip inward at this point?"

Sheridan placed the palm of her empty hand to her forehead. "What kind of question is that?"

"Think," he snapped back.

She could see the seriousness in his eyes. "The back of the house goes straight across."

"Thank you," he responded. "I didn't mean to snap at you."

She knew his apology was sincere. "Please tell me what is going on."

David's eyes met hers. He could see the anger and confusion in them. She was angry because her father had cheated on her mother. What she didn't know was he cheated on her mother with his mother. And that he was really her half-brother. David didn't know quite how he was going to tell her the rest of the story. His main concern right now was finding out what was behind this wine rack. "Look," he said as he pointed a beam of light to the protruding wall. "If the back of the house is straight across, then what is behind this part of the wine rack?"

Sheridan looked at the wall, trying to recollect anything from her past that might answer his question. After a minute, she locked eyes with his. "Why should I care what it is? I'm more concerned about what my father has done and what I'm going to do about it. Why does this wall matter to you?"

David quickly retrieved the bottle of Amber Wine, handing it to her while holding the beam of light on the label. "This is why. This is a sign...I just know it." He pointed. "Read the label."

Sheridan stared at the label, shaking her head. "I don't get it."

David jerked his finger, landing it on the word Amber. "Right there...Amber, as in amber wine. And the year 1986...that was the year Amber Paige went missing after the affair with your father. She was pregnant with his child. And that was a threat to his career." He turned to the wine rack, placing both hands on it, staring through it to the wall behind. "I think she is here…my mother is here." He didn't even realize the word mother had slipped out.

"Your what!" she shouted.

Chapter 45

David snapped to attention. Her sharp tone triggered his memory. The cat was out of the bag. He slowly turned, facing her. Sheridan frowned through teary eyes. "That is what I was about to tell you upstairs," David said in a calm even voice. "David Peoples is my undercover name. My real name is David Paige. And my mother is Amber Paige."

"And your father?" she spat out instantly, but already knew the answer.

David stared into her glassy eyes.

"Don't lie to me," she said in a shaky voice.

"Other than my name...I have never lied to you, with words or my feelings," he responded. "It wasn't until late last night that I found out who my real father is...Robert Blakely."

The sound of her father's name flushed out her tears. Sheridan buried her face in her hands as she turned away. David stepped to her, placing a comforting hand on her shoulder. "I wish it wasn't true."

She sniffed and wiped her eyes, still not facing him. "Do you remember last weekend?"

"How could I not?" he replied. "It was the best weekend of my life. That is the truth."

She turned, giving him a wet smile. "It was mine too."

"I need your help," he said as he wiped her tears. "I have got to find out what happened to my mother. And there is something behind this wall that I believe will help me find her."

"Are you still going to help me find my mother?"

"Of course," he replied. "It's even more important to me now than ever."

She rendered him a smile. "How can I help?"

"Take the rest of the wine bottles out…I will look for a crowbar."

Sheridan began pulling out bottles and standing them on the floor nearby. David went to the other part of the cellar where he remembered seeing tools hanging on shadow boards. He grabbed a crowbar and claw hammer. By the time he returned to Sheridan, she had the wall rack emptied. David sunk the teeth of the crowbar into the oak board where it was nailed. He pulled on the long handle, freeing the rack from the wall. Creaking sounds echoed in the cellar as he disassembled the rack. After moving the loose parts out of his way, he began prying the wide oak boards from the wall. He worked steadily with Sheridan helping by his side, as if she had a stake in what was behind this wall. Each board sounded with a heavy thud as it struck the floor below. Behind the wide oak boards was a door. The door knob was broken off to make it flush with the wall. With a finger buried in the crack of the door, David attempted to pull it open. It was locked with no apparent key. He did not hesitate as he sank the teeth of the crowbar into the crack. He jerked the long handle, popping the door open a crack.

David and Sheridan locked eyes; anticipation filled their faces. Dust from their work clouded the room, giving the light an amber glow. David dropped the crowbar to the ground and grabbed the door with both hands. He grunted as he struggled to pry it open, moving it only a fraction. Sheridan stepped in and they both took hold of the door. With precise synchronization they pulled; the door slowly opened, creaking loudly on extremely rusted hinges. The lights blinked on and off several times as the door opened completely.

They both stood in front of the doorway, with air cold as ice drifting from within. David took his penlight, piercing the darkness with its narrow beam. Before them appeared to be a small cavity dug into the ground, about eight foot deep and ten foot square. David dropped the beam to his feet, revealing that a set of steps leading downward into the room had been busted up, apparently on purpose. David remembered seeing a ladder in the tool area of the cellar. He rushed to get it. As he turned back, a green Coleman lantern caught his eye. He picked it up and gently wiggled it to see if there was gas in its tank. He smiled as he felt it slosh, about half-full he guessed. He then searched for matches and found some tucked away in the corner of a drawer.

David returned with the ladder and lantern. Sheridan helped him lower one end of the ladder to the floor below. David took the lantern and pumped the pressure up tight. He then pulled out a stick match and dragged the tip along the metal side of the ladder. A long thin flame spurred from the ladder. He carefully inserted the small flame into the lantern just beneath two white sacks. He cracked the gas line and two blue flames instantly lit within the two white sacks. He removed the match and gently turned the knob for the gas line. The old lantern roared to life, illuminating the entire cellar.

They both squinted from the intense light. David took it up by its handle and held it out into the dark cavity. The tiny room lit up, revealing nothing inside. "How old is this house?" David asked.

"My grandfather bought the land and rebuilt over the original house that had burnt down from the previous owner."

"Was the original house built before 1900?" he asked.

Sheridan hesitated. "I believe the original house was built just before the Civil War...why?"

"I believe this is an ice room," David said as he peered into the room again. "In the old days people would carve out rooms deep in the ground where they would store their ice in blocks."

Sheridan peered into the room. "That's probably what this is. It's freezing in there. But I don't see anything but dirt."

"There must be a clue in there somewhere," David said as he turned and stepped onto the ladder. "I have to take a look."

He carefully lowered himself down the steep ladder, holding the lantern in one hand. Sheridan followed out of curiosity. The lantern illuminated the small room as if the sun had burst onto the scene. The air was frigid, their breath visible. David walked slowly around the room, studying the walls for some type of clue.

"There is nothing down here but three stones," Sheridan said, shivering. "It's freezing. Let's get out of here."

David concentrated on the walls, still searching for the next clue, ignoring her request. Then suddenly he stopped and turned to her. "Three what?"

Sheridan pointed to the bare dirt floor. "There are three stones down here and nothing else."

David looked down at the floor. He had paid no attention to it before. She was right—along one edge sat three stones the size of golf balls, evenly spaced about four feet apart. David's eyes narrowed as he stared at the three stones. Then his eyes grew wide, shock flushing his face. "Oh hell," he said as he turned and began climbing up the ladder.

"What is it, David?" she asked, seeing the shocked expression on his face.

"I have to get something. I'll be right back."

David was back as quickly as he had said. Sheridan watched him climb down the ladder with a shovel in one hand.

"Oh my God… David, you don't think…"

David cut her sentence short, knowing what she was thinking. "Yes I do. I can feel it in my bones." Then their eyes met. "No pun intended."

David went straight to the stone to his left, as if mysteriously drawn to the spot. He sank the point of the shovel into the soil two feet below the stone. The soil was packed but easily removed. After about two feet, David felt the point of the shovel strike something beneath the surface. It wasn't hard like rock, but softer and springy. He carefully dug around the spot, not wanting to damage what was below. Gradually something black appeared through the loose dirt. As David worked the dirt, it became apparent that it was a plastic trash bag, large like a leaf bag.

David stopped digging and stuck the end of the shovel in the ground out of the way nearby. Sheridan moved the lantern closer, as David dropped to a knee and brushed off a spot about three feet long. He pulled a small pocket knife out of his pocket. Carefully he cut a shallow seam through the plastic. With both hands he opened the black plastic bag. There was an unrecognizable skeleton before him, but he recognized the red dress and the strands of long blonde hair.

"David…is that?"

David suddenly felt a tingling sensation throughout his body. He clamped his eyes shut as the sensation chilled his soul. Tears squeezed through his closed lids; a sweet sensation lingered.

"Yes," he replied in a sad voice.

"I am so sorry," she said sincerely, placing a comforting hand on his head. "David…you are trembling."

He raised his tear-stained eyes to her. "She just touched my soul…I think she is happy now and finally at peace."

Tears filled Sheridan's eyes. "This is unbelievable. I am sad but so happy for you."

David looked deeply into her eyes. "Are you all right? You know what this means."

Sheridan nodded, and hatred spilled from her eyes. "Yes, my…our father is a murderer."

David knew for sure at that instant that she did not love her father. He was looking into scornful eyes, not sorrowful ones. He straightened up, grabbed the shovel, and went to the next stone. He dug down into the earth at the point below the stone equal to the last. At the same depth his shovel struck another soft object. Like the other, he cleared away a spot about three feet long. He opened the black plastic bag, revealing skeletal remains and auburn hair.

"I wonder who she was," Sheridan said. "Probably another mistress."

David recognized the auburn hair from pictures of Angela and Amber together. "I don't think so. I believe this was my mother's roommate, Angela Graham. She filed the missing person report on my mother. He was covering his own tracks."

"What kind of monster is he?" she asked, then turned to look at the third stone. Sheridan did not say a word, but only stared at the stone, as tears streamed down her cheeks. David noticed her stare and her tears; she must be having the same thoughts as he. Without a word, he rose and moved to the third stone. Again about two feet down, the shovel struck another soft object. He moved back the dirt, revealing another black plastic bag. He glanced up at her and saw tears flowing down her cheeks. "Are you ready?"

Sheridan silently nodded. David slowly opened the bag. A bony hand fell out. A ring rolled off a finger and came to rest in loose dirt. David picked up the ring and noticed writing engraved on the inside. He drew it closer to his eyes and read the inscription: With all my love, Sheridan. David's eyes quickly rose to meet Sheridan's. Her hands were covering her mouth, shock cast over her face. She recognized the ring she had given her mother. David placed it in her hand as she broke down in tears. Suddenly she shut her eyes and sucked in a deep breath, as if something just grabbed her. She began to tremble as more tears streamed down her cheeks. "Mother…I can feel her."

David held her in his arms as they both wept.

Chapter 46

Cooper Union in New York City is a historic meeting place. Great presidents of the past gave great speeches from the Great Hall podium. Ironically President Lincoln gave his historic "Right Makes Might" speech here. On this blustery Sunday evening, a Senator presumed to be a president in the near future was giving a speech to a room filled mostly with women. Ironically he was delivering a speech on Women's Rights, how women are still being overlooked and mistreated in this still male-dominated corporate nation.

Senator Robert Blakely stood tall and proud behind the Great Hall podium. Many men much greater than he had stood there before, but none holding a greater secret. He looked out over the vast crowd before him, eager young and wiser older faces drinking in every word that spilled from his lips. He was performing a flawless speech, king of his audience. Unknown to him and his subjects before him, his kingdom was about to come crashing down, witnessed by the eyes of many women.

Just after Senator Robert Blakely had begun his final performance, a dozen or more squad cars had silently lined the perimeter of Cooper Union. Uniforms entered from all directions, while David, Sheridan, and Moreno entered the front. This red brick architectural masterpiece that had seen more than its share of historic events was about to witness another piece of history. Though this event will probably never be written in any valid history book, it most definitely will capture the headlines of the major newspapers and be archived forever.

Senator Robert Blakely was at the height of his performance when he observed movement along the outer walls of the room. He watched as the usual number of policemen doubled, then tripled. Blakely's peripheral vision detected movement to his rear. He stopped speaking momentarily as he reached for a nearby glass of water. As if quenching his thirst, he raised the glass and tilted it against his lips while he slightly turned his head to claim a better view. Moreno and two uniformed cops were gathered behind him, waiting, like cats preparing to pounce on their prey.

Blakely knew Moreno only by name, not appearance, so he glared at the supposed stranger, a man with a swollen and bandaged face. Moreno wasn't even supposed to be working, but had gotten special permission from Lieutenant Jacoby to make the arrest since Blakely was the one responsible for Moreno's near-death experience. While Blakely's attention was to his rear, he heard his once-captivated audience to his front murmuring. He turned back just in time to see David and Sheridan approaching. "Sheridan darling," Blakely said while his eyes darted to David. "What is the meaning of this?"

"I know what you did to Mother," she blurted out in anger.

Blakely's eyes cut even deeper into David. "This man must be feeding you a pack of lies."

"This man has a name," David threw back at Blakely.

"I know who you are, Mr. Peoples. And I know what you are." Blakely's eyes fell back upon Sheridan, his only child, so he thought.

"My name is not Peoples," David said, capturing Blakely's attention. "My name is David Paige," he said proudly as Blakely's eyes widened. "My mother is Amber Paige."

Blakely stood stunned in disbelief. David held out a piece of the red dress his mother had worn. "And I know what you did to my mother."

Sheridan held out a hand, her mother's ring resting softly in her palm. "And I know what you did to Mother."

Two uniformed cops stepped up, cuffing a shell-shocked Robert Blakely from behind. Blakely did not resist, only stood still as if rooted, staring back and forth into his children's angry eyes. Moreno stepped up as well, reading him his rights he knew by heart. "Robert Blakely...you are under arrest for the murders of Amber Paige...Patricia Blakely...and Angela Graham."

Moreno continued reading Blakely his rights. Blakely ignored them and stared into David's like eyes. "You are my son?"

David matched his stare. "Not any longer...my father died the day he murdered my mother."

"Same here," Sheridan exclaimed as they took Robert Blakely away in cuffs.

Three weeks passed. Robert Blakely was facing multiple ironclad cases of murder in the first degree. His own daughter, Sheridan, had mounted a campaign of her own to destroy her father. After the evidence against Robert Blakely had been gathered, Sheridan took her mother's remains and gave her a proper burial. David attended the ceremony by Sheridan's invitation. They were in mutual agreement to stay in close touch, but to keep their brief love affair a secret. David promised to visit and someday bring Kimberly to New York City to see the sights and meet his new sister. Sheridan beamed at the thought of someday meeting her opposition. David didn't have the heart to tell Sheridan that he had already chosen Kimberly over her even before he discovered their relation.

David also had personally seen that Angela Graham's remains were delivered to her sister, Victoria Cromwell. He attended her ceremony as well, where Angela Graham was laid to rest in their family cemetery. Victoria was very thankful for everything David had done. Though the realization of Angela's death was devastating to the family, they could now begin to heal.

David then took his own mother's remains to a place she had never been—Mount Pleasant in sunny

South Carolina, where her baby boy had been safely hidden from the evil monster who murdered her. One of the many definitions of a mother is one who makes sacrifices for her child. Amber Paige had been the best mother she could have been by giving the ultimate sacrifice, her own life, to save David's. Now her haunted soul was laid to rest beside her twin sister Alice, who was also the best mother she could have been to David.

On Sunday, New Year's Day, David and Kimberly stood in front of the double headstone monument, like the ones designed for a husband and wife. It pictured twin lady angels holding two intertwined hearts with names on each. In large bold letters deeply engraved near the top center was PAIGE. On the left heart was the name Alice, with her life dates inscribed below. On the right heart was the name Amber, with her life dates inscribed below as well. Inscribed across the bottom was a phrase that read: Here rests a pair of twin angels, Alice and Amber, their lives inseparable from the moment of birth. Then time separated them for years, only to be reunited after death. They were two loving mothers sharing a single common goal, a mutual son. This son remains very thankful for their undying love.

"That is a beautiful memorial," Kimberly said with tear-filled eyes, admiring the double-angel headstone. "Where did you find that phrase?"

David grinned. "I found it in my head."

She looked at him puzzled and somewhat amazed. "It just doesn't sound like something you would come up with."

"I'm not the same man I once was."

Kimberly gazed into his deep blue eyes, thinking that his statement was reminiscent of someone returning from war. She was well aware of his battles and struggles the past two months, but she was not aware of the battle within his heart. She squeezed his hand. "You have been through a lot these past two months."

David gazed straight ahead at the breathtaking angel headstone. "My world has been turned upside down. The only mother that I have known and loved suddenly died. Then I came to find out she wasn't my biological mother; her sister was. While searching for my long-lost mother I came face to face with death. Luckily I walked away with only a stab wound." David turned and met her gaze. "I think I have matured in years over the past two months. I find myself thinking of my future more than ever before."

Kimberly gave him her full attention, never hearing him speak this way before. "So tell me…what lies ahead in the next chapter of David Paige's life?"

David could feel the warmth of her stare as his eyes rested back on the memorial. "I think I have come to a point in my life where I need to make roots…and begin planting seeds."

Kimberly's eyes watered, her heart swelled. These were the words she had yearned to hear him say for a long time.

David turned to her as her glassy eyes beamed. "And I know who I want to share the rest of my life with."

Her eyes couldn't hold back the tears of joy any longer as she and David melted into each other's arms.